COLOUR

Acclaim for Leila Aboulela's *The Translator*

'A story of love and faith all the more moving for the restraint with which it is written.'

J. M. Coetzee, Booker Prize Winner 1999

'. . . a lyrical journey about exile, loss and love . . . poetry in motion.'

The Sunday Times

'Aboulela is a wonderfully poetic writer: it's a pleasure to read a novel so full of feeling and yet so serene.'

The Guardian

'. . . she pulls you into her world as she refracts British life, its smells and sounds, its advertisements and turns of phrase . . .'

The Independent

'. . . [an] extraordinary first novel . . .'

The Herald

'. . . the first halal novel written in English!'

The Muslim News

'*The Translator* is an enveloping story of the tentative possibilities between a man and a woman, and between faiths; two people, and perhaps peoples, between nations. It is an apt, resonant caution filled with love and poignant understanding of the world. It is exactly what fiction ought to be.'

Todd McEwen

Coloured Lights

Leila Aboulela

First published in 2001
New edition published in 2005 by Polygon an imprint of Birlinn Ltd
West Newington House
10 Newington Road
Edinburgh
www.birlinn.co.uk

© Leila Aboulela, 2001, 2005
Typeset by Hewer Text Ltd, Edinburgh, and
printed and bound in Great Britain by
Creative Print & Design, Ebbw Vale, Wales

A CIP Record for this book is
available from the British Library

ISBN 10: 1 904598 53 6
ISBN 13: 978 1 904598 53 4

The right of Leila Aboulela
to be identified as author of this work
has been asserted in accordance with
the Copyright, Designs and Patents Act 1988.

The publishers acknowledge subsidy from the
Scottish Arts Council towards the publication of this volume.

For my teachers – my mother and father

Contents

Coloured Lights

I cried a little as the bus started to fill up with people in Charing Cross Road and passed the stone lions in Trafalgar Square. Not proper crying with sobs and moans but a few silly tears and water dribbling from my nose. It was not the West Indian conductor who checked my pass that day but a young boy who looked bored. The West Indian conductor is very friendly with me; he tells me I look like one of his daughters and that he wants one day to visit the Sudan, to see Africa for the first time. When I tell him of our bread queues and sugar coupons, he looks embarrassed and leaves me to collect the fares of other passengers. I was crying for Taha or maybe because I was homesick, not only for my daughters or my family but sick with longing for the heat, the sweat and the water of the Nile. The English word 'homesick' is a good one; we do not have exactly the same word in Arabic. In Arabic my state would have been described as 'yearning for the homeland' or the 'sorrow of alienation' and there is also truth in this. I was alienated from this place where darkness descended unnaturally at 4 pm and people went about their business as if nothing had happened.

I was in a country which Taha had never visited and yet his memory was closer to me than it had been for years. Perhaps it was my new solitude, perhaps he came to me in dreams I could not

1

recall. Or was my mind reeling from the newness surrounding me? I was in London on a one-year contract with the BBC World Service. Each day as I read the news in Arabic, my voice, cool and distant, reached my husband in Kuwait, and my parents who were looking after my daughters in Khartoum.

Now I was older than Taha had been when he died. At that time he was ten years older than me and like my other brothers he had humoured me and spoiled me. When he died, my mind bent a little and has never straightened since. How could a young mind absorb the sudden death of a brother on the day of his wedding? It seemed at first to be a ghastly mistake, but that was an illusion, a mirage. The Angel of Death makes no mistakes. He is a reliable servant who never fails to keep his appointment at the predetermined time and place. Taha had no premonition of his own death. He was fidgety, impatient but not for that, not for the end coming so soon. It was too painful to think of what must have been his own shock, his own useless struggle against the inevitable. Nor did anyone else have foreknowledge. How could we, when we were steeped in wedding preparations and our house was full of relatives helping with the wedding meal?

From the misty windows I saw the words 'Gulf Air' written in Arabic and English on the doors of the airline's office and imagined myself one day buying a ticket to go to Hamid in Kuwait. It seemed that the fate of our generation is separation, from our country or our family. We are ready to go anywhere in search of the work we cannot find at home. Hamid says that there are many Sudanese in Kuwait and he hopes that in the next year or so the girls and I will join him. Every week, I talk to him on the telephone, long leisurely conversations. We run up huge telephone bills but seem to be unable to ration our talking. He tells me amusing stories of the emirs whose horses he cures. In Sudan, cattle die from starvation or disease all the time, cattle which are the livelihood of many people. But one of the country's few veterinary surgeons is away, working with animals whose purpose is only to amuse. Why? So that his daughters can have a good education, so that he can keep up with the latest research in his field. So that he can justify the years of his life spent in education by earning the salary he deserves. And I thought of Taha's short life and wondered.

In Regent Street the conductor had to shake himself from his lethargy and prevent more people from boarding the bus. The progress of the bus was slow in contrast to the shoppers who swarmed around in the brightly lit streets. Every shop window boasted an innovative display and there were new decorative lights in addition to the street lights. Lights twined around the short trees on the pavements, on wires stretched across the street. Festive December lights. Blue, red, green lights, more elaborate than the crude strings of bulbs that we use in Khartoum to decorate the wedding house.

But the lights for Taha's wedding did not shine as they were meant to on that night. By the time night came he was already buried and we were mourning, not celebrating. Over the period of mourning, the wedding dinner was gradually eaten by visitors. The women indoors, sitting on mattresses spread on the floors, the men on wobbling metal chairs in a tent pitched in front of our house, the dust of the street under their feet. But they drank water and tea and not the sweet orange squash my mother and her friends had prepared by boiling small oranges with sugar. That went to a neighbour who was bold enough to enquire about it. Her children carried the sweet liquid from our house in large plastic bottles, their eyes bright, their lips moist with expectation.

When Taha died I felt raw and I remained transparent for a long time. Death had come so close to me that I was almost exhilarated; I could see clearly that not only life but the world is transient. But with time my heart hardened and I became immersed in the cares

3

of day-to-day life. I had become detached from this vulnerable feeling and it was good to recapture it now and grieve once again.

Taha's life: I was not there for a large part of it but I remember the time he got engaged and my own secret feelings of jealousy towards his fiancée. Muddled feelings of admiration and a desire to please. She was a university student and to my young eyes she seemed so articulate and self-assured. I remember visiting her room in the university hostels while Taha waited for us outside by the gate, hands in his pockets, making patterns in the dust with his feet. Her room was lively, in disarray with clothes and shoes scattered about and colourful posters on the wall. It was full of chatting room-mates and friends who kept coming in and out to eat the last biscuits in the open packet on the desk, borrow the prayer mat or dab their eyes with kohl from a silver flask. They scrutinised my face for any likeness to Taha, laughed at jokes I could not understand, while I sat nervously on the edge of a bed, smiling and unable to speak. Later with Taha we went to a concert in the football grounds where a group of students sang. I felt very moved by a song in the form of a letter written by a political prisoner to his mother. Taha's bride afterwards wrote the words out for me, humming the tune, looking radiant and Taha remarked on how elegant her handwriting was.

In the shop windows dummies posed, aloof strangers in the frenzied life of Oxford Street. Wools, rich silks and satin dresses. 'Taha, shall I wear tonight the pink or the green?' I asked him on the morning of the wedding. 'See, I look like–like a watermelon in this green.' His room was an extension of the house where a verandah used to be, a window from the hall still looked into it, the door was made of shutters. He never slept in his room. In the early evening we all dragged our beds outdoors so that the sheets were cool when it was time to gaze up at the stars. If it rained Taha did not care, he covered his head with the sheet and continued to sleep. When the dust came thickly, I would shake his shoulder to wake him up to go indoors and he would shout at me to leave him alone. In the morning his hair would be covered with dust, sand in his ears, his eyelashes. He would sneeze and blame me for not insisting, for failing to get him to move inside.

He smiled at me in my green dress; his suitcase half-filled lay open on the floor; he leaned against the shutters holding them shut with his weight. Through them filtered the hisses and smells of frying, the clinking of empty water glasses scented with incense and the thud of a hammer on a slab of ice, the angry splinters flying in the air, disintegrating, melting in surrender when they greeted the warm floor. Someone was calling him, an aunt cupped a hand round her mouth, tongue strong and dancing from side to side she trilled the ululation, the joy cry. When others joined her the sound rose in waves to fill the whole house. Was it a tape or was it someone singing that silly song 'Our Bridegroom like Honey? Where can you ever find another like him?' To answer my question about the dress, he told me words I knew to be absurd but wanted to believe. 'Tonight you will look more beautiful than the bride.'

The bus headed north and we passed Regent's Park and the Central Mosque; all was peaceful and dark after the congestion of the shopping centre. I was glad that there were no more coloured lights, for they are cheerful but false. I had held others like them before in my hands, wiping the dust off each bulb and saying to Taha, 'How could you have taken them from the electrician when they were so dusty?' And he had helped me clean them with an orange cloth that he used for the car because he was in a hurry to set them up all around the outside of the house. I had teased him saying that the colours were not in an ordered pattern. We laughed together trying to make sense of their order, but they were random, chaotic. Then Hamid, who was his friend, arrived and said he would help him set them up. I asked Taha to get me a present from Nairobi, where he was going for his honeymoon, and Hamid had looked, directly at me, laughed in his easy way and said without hiding his envy, 'He is not going to have time to get you any presents.' At that time, Hamid and I were not even engaged and I felt shy from his words and walked away from his gaze.

It was the lights that killed Taha. The haphazard, worn strings of lights that had been hired out for years to house after wedding house. A bare live wire carelessly touched. A rushed drive to the hospital where I watched a stray cat twist and rub its thin body around the legs of our bridegroom's death bed. And in the crowded corridors, people squatted on the floor and the screams for Taha were absorbed by the dirty walls, the listless flies and the generous, who had space and tears for a stranger they had never met before.

My mother, always a believing woman, wailed and wept but did not pour dirt on her head or tear her clothes like some ignorant women do. She just kept saying again and again, 'I wish I never lived to see this day.' Perhaps Hamid had the greatest shock, for he was with Taha when he was setting up the lights. Later he told me that when they buried Taha he had stayed at the graveside after the other men had gone. He had prayed to strengthen his friend's soul at its crucial moment of questioning. The moment in the grave, in the interspace between death and eternity when the Angels ask the soul 'Who is your lord?' and there must be no wavering in the reply, no saying 'I don't know.' The answer must come swiftly with confidence and it was for this assurance, in the middle of what must have been Taha's fear, that Hamid prayed.

I had been in London for nearly seven months and I told no one about Taha. I felt that it would sound distasteful or like a bad joke, but electricity had killed others in Khartoum too, though I did not know them personally. A young boy once urinated at the foot of a lamp light which had a base from which wires stuck out, exposed. A girl in my school was cleaning a fridge, squatting barefoot in a puddle of melted ice with the electric socket too close. The girl's younger sister was in my class and the whole class, forty girls, went in the school bus to visit the family at home. On the way we sang songs as if we were on a school picnic and I cannot help but remember that day with pleasure.

With time, the relationship between my family and Taha's bride soured. Carefully prepared dishes ceased to pass between my mother and hers. In the two Eids, during which we celebrated in one the end of the fasting month of Ramadan and in the other the feast of sacrifice, our families no longer visited. Out of a sense of duty, my parents had proposed that she marry another of my brothers but she and her family refused. Instead she married one of her cousins who was not very educated, not as much as Taha at any rate. Sometimes, I would see her in the streets of Khartoum with her children and we would only greet each other if our eyes met.

In Taha's memory, my father built a small school in his home village on the Blue Nile. One classroom built of mud to teach young children to read and write. The best charity for the dead is something continuous that goes on yielding benefit over time. But like other schools it kept running into difficulties: no books, costly paper, poor attendance when children were sometimes kept at home to help their parents. Yet my father persevered and the school had become something of a hobby for him in his retirement. It is also a good excuse for him to travel frequently from the capital to the village and visit his old friends and family. What my mother did for Taha was more simple. She bought a *zeer*, a large clay pot and had it fastened to a tree in front of our house. The *zeer* held water, keeping it cool and it was covered by a round piece of wood on which stood a tin mug for drinking. Early in the morning, I would fill it with water from the fridge and throughout the day passers-by, hot and thirsty from the glaring sun, could drink, resting in the shade of the tree. In London, I came across the same idea, memorial benches placed in gardens and parks where people could rest. My mother would never believe that anyone would voluntarily sit in the sun but then she had never seen cold, dark evenings like these.

It was time for me to get off the bus as we had long passed Lords Cricket Grounds, Swiss Cottage and Golders Green. My stop was near the end of the route and there were only a few passengers left. After dropping me off, the bus would turn around to resume its cycle. My grief for Taha comes in cycles as well, over the years, rising and receding. Like the appearance of the West Indian conductor, it is transient and difficult to predict. Perhaps he will be on the bus tomorrow evening. 'Like them Christmas lights?' he will ask, and, grateful to see a familiar face amidst the alien darkness and cold, I will say, 'Yes, I admire the coloured lights.'

Souvenirs

They set out early, before sunset. Not the right time for visiting, but it was going to be a long drive and his sister Manaal said she would not be able to recognise the painter's house in the dark. The car slipped from the shaded car-port into the white sunlight of the afternoon, the streets were empty, their silence reminiscent of dawn.

Since he had come on the plane from Scotland two weeks ago, Yassir had not gone out at this time of day. Instead he had rested after lunch wearing his old jellabia. He would lie on one of the beds that were against the walls of the sitting room, playing with a toothpick in his mouth and talking to Manaal without looking at her. On the bed perpendicular to his, she would lie with her feet near his head so that had they been children she might have reached out and pulled his hair with her toes. And the child Yassir would have let his heels graze the white wall leaving brown stains for which he would be punished later. Now they talked slowly, probing for common interests and so remembering things past, gossiping lightly about others, while all the time the air cooler blew the edges of the bedsheets just a little, intermittently, and the smells of lunch receded. Then the air cooler's sound would take over, dominate the room, blowing their thoughts away and they would sleep until the time came when all the garden was in shade.

In this respect, Yassir had slotted easily into the life of Khartoum, after five years on the North Sea oil-rigs, noisy helicopter flights to and from Dyce airport, a grey sea with waves as crazy as the sky. Five years of two weeks off-shore, two weeks on with Emma in Aberdeen. No naps after lunch there and yet he could here lie and know that the rhythms the air cooler whispered into his heart were familiar, well known. When he had first arrived he had put fresh straw into the air cooler's box. Standing outdoors on an upturned Pepsi crate, he had wedged open the grimy perforated frame with a screwdriver, unleashed cobwebs and plenty of dust: fresh powdery dust and solid fluffs that had lost all resemblance to sand. The old bale of straw had shrunk over the years, gone dark and rigid from the constant exposure to water. He oiled the water pump and put in the new bale of straw. Its smell filled the house for days, the air that blew out was cooler. For this his mother had thanked him and like other times before, prayed that he would only find good people in his path. It was true, he was always fortunate in the connections he made, in the people who held the ability to further his interests. In the past teachers, now his boss, his colleagues, Emma.

But 'Your wife – what's her name?' was how his mother referred to Emma. She would not say Emma's name. She would not 'remember' it. It would have been the same if Emma had been Jane, Alison or Susan, any woman from 'outside'. Outside that large pool of names his mother knew and could relate to. That was his punishment, nothing more, nothing less. He accepted it as the nomad bears the times of drought which come to starve his cattle, biding time, waiting for the tightness to run its course and the rain that must eventually fall. Manaal would smile in an embarrassed way when their mother said that. And as if time had dissolved the age gap between them, she would attempt a faint defence. 'Leave him alone, Mama,' she would say, in a whisper, avoiding their eyes, wary, lest her words instead of calming, provoked the much feared outburst. Manaal had met Emma two years ago in Aberdeen. What she had told his mother about Emma, what she had said to try to drive away the rejection that gripped her, he didn't know.

For Yassir, Emma was Aberdeen. Unbroken land after the sea. Real life after the straight lines of the oil-rig. A kind of freedom. Before Emma his leave on-shore had floated, never living up to his expectations. And it was essential for those who worked on the rigs that those on-shore days were fulfilling enough to justify the hardship of the rigs. A certain formula was needed, a certain balance which evaded him. Until one day he visited the dentist for two fillings and, with lips frozen with procaine, read out loud the name, Emma, written in Arabic, on a golden necklace that hung around the receptionist's throat.

'Your wife – what's her name?' his mother says as if clumsily smudging out a fact, hurting it. A fact, a history: three years ago he drove Emma to the maternity ward in Foresterhill, in the middle of a summer's night that looked like twilight, to deliver a daughter who did not make her appearance until the afternoon of the following day. Samia changed in the two weeks that he did not see her. Her growth marked time like nothing else did. Two weeks off-shore, two weeks with Emma and Samia, two weeks off-shore again, Emma driving him to the heliport, the child in her own seat at the back. A fact, a history. Yet here, when Manaal's friends visited, some with toddlers, some with good jobs, careers, there was a 'see what you've missed' atmosphere around the house. An atmosphere that was neither jocular nor of regret. So that he had come to realise, with the sick bleakness that accompanies truth, that his mother imagined that he could just leave Emma and leave the child, come home, and those five years would have been just an aberration, time forgotten. He could marry one of Manaal's friends, one who would not mind that he had been married before, that he had left behind a child somewhere in Europe. A bride who would regard all that as a man's experience. When talking to her friends she would say the word 'experienced' in a certain way, smiling secretly.

Because the streets were silent, Yassir and Manaal were silent too, as if by talking they would disturb those who were resting indoors. Yassir drove slowly, pebbles spat out from under the wheels, he was careful to avoid the potholes. The windows wide open let in dust but closing them would be suffocating. From their house in Safia they crossed the bridge into Khartoum and it was busier there, more cars, more people walking in the streets. That part of the journey, the entry into Khartoum reminded him of the Blue Nile Cinema, which was a little way under the bridge. He remembered as a student walking back from the cinema, late at night to the Barracks, as his hostel was called, because it was once army barracks. He used to walk with his friends in a kind of swollen high, full of the film he had just seen. Films like *A Man for All Seasons, Educating Rita, Chariots of Fire*.

There was still a long way for them to go, past the Extension, beyond the airport, past Riyadh to the newly built areas of Taif and El-Ma'moura. Not a very practical idea, a drain of the week's ration of petrol and there was the possibility that the painter would not be in and the whole journey would have been wasted. Manaal was optimistic though. 'They'll be in,' she said, *'Insha Allah*. Especially if we get there early enough before they go out anywhere.' There were no telephones in El-Ma'moura, it was a newly built area with no street numbers, no addresses.

That morning, he had mentioned buying a painting or two to take back to Aberdeen and Manaal had suggested Ronan K. He was English; his wife gave private English lessons (Manaal was once her student). Now in the car when he asked more about him she said, 'For years he sat doing nothing, he had no job, maybe he was painting. I didn't know about that until the Hilton commissioned him to do some paintings for the cafeteria. No one knows why this couple live here. They are either crazy or they are spies. Everyone thinks they are spies.'

'You all like to think these sensational things,' he said. 'What is there to spy on anyway?'

'They're nice though,' she said. 'I hope they are not spies.' Yassir shook his head, thinking it was hopeless to talk sense to her.

The paintings were not his idea, they were Emma's. Emma was good with ideas, new suggestions, it was one of the things he admired about her. Yassir didn't know much about painting. If he walked into a room he would not notice the paintings on the wall and he secretly thought they were an extravagance. But then he felt like that about many of the things Emma bought. What he considered luxuries, she considered necessities. Like the Bambi wallpaper in Samia's room must be bought to match the curtains, which match the bedspread, which match Thumper on the pillow-case. And there was a Bambi video, a Ladybird book, a pop-up book. He would grumble but she would persuade him. She would say that as a child she had cried in the cinema when Bambi's mother was shot. Popcorn could not stop the tears, the nasal flood. Of pop-up books and Halloween costumes, she would say, as a child I had these things. He would think, 'I didn't.'

This time Emma had asked, 'What can you get from Khartoum for the house?' They were eating muesli and watching Mr Motivator on GMTV. Mr M had a litre and a half of bottled mineral water in each hand. He was using them as weights while he squatted down and up, down and up, *Knees over your toes*. The labels on the bottles had been slyly removed.

'Nothing. There's nothing there,' Yassir said.

'What do tourists get when they go there?'

'Tourists don't go there,' he said. 'It's not a touristy place. The only foreigners there are working.' Once when Yassir was in

University he had met a British journalist. The journalist was wearing shorts which looked comical because no one else wore shorts unless they were playing sports. He had chatted to Yassir and some of his friends.

'There must be something you can get,' Emma said. 'Things carved in wood, baskets . . .'

'There's a shop which sell ivory things. Elephants made of ivory and things like that.'

'No. Not ivory.'

'I could get you a handbag made of crocodile skin?'

'No, yuck.'

'Snake skin?'

'Stop it, I'm serious.'

'Ostrich feathers?'

'NO DEAD ANIMALS. Think of something else.'

'There's a bead market. Someone once told me about that. I don't know where it is though. I'll have to find out.'

'If you get me beads I can have them made here into a necklace.' Emma liked necklaces but not bracelets or earrings. The golden necklace with her name in Arabic was from an ex-boyfriend, a mud-logger who had been working rotational from the oil-rigs in Oman.

'Change your mind and come with me. You can take the Malaria pills, Samia can take the syrup and it's just a few vaccines . . .'

'A few jabs! Typhoid, yellow fever, cholera, TB! And Samia might get bitten by this sandfly Manaal told us about when she came here. She is only three. It's not worth it – maybe when she's older . . .'

'You're not curious to see where I grew up?'

'I am interested a bit but – I don't know – I've never heard anything good about that place.'

'This is just a two-week holiday, that's all. My mother will get to see you and Samia, you'll have a look around . . .' he said switching Mr Motivator off.

'Paintings,' she said, 'that's what you should get. You can bring back paintings of all those things you think I should be curious about. Or just take lots of photographs and bring the beads.'

He bought the beads but did not take any photographs. He had shied away from that, as if unable to click a camera at his house, his old school, the cinemas that brought the sparkle of life abroad. So when Manaal said she knew this English painter, he was enthusiastic about the idea even though it was his last evening in Khartoum. Tomorrow his flight would leave for home. He hoped he would have with him some paintings for Emma. She would care about where each one went, on this wall or that. She cared about things more than he did. She even cared about Samia more than he did. Emma was in tune with the child's every burp and whimper. In comparison to Emma, Yassir's feelings for Samia were jammed up, unable to flow. Sometimes with the two of them he felt himself dispensable, he thought they could manage without him. They did just that when he was off-shore. They had a life together; playgroup, kindergym, Duthie Park. When Manaal came to Aberdeen she said many times, 'Emma is so good with the child. She talks to her as if she is an adult.'

Yassir now wondered, as they drove down Airport Road, if Manaal had said such positive things to his mother. Or if she had only told of the first day of her visit to Aberdeen. The day she reached out to hold the sleeping child and Emma said, 'No, I'd rather you didn't. She'll be frightened if she wakes up and finds a stranger holding her.' The expression on Manaal's face had lingered throughout the whole visit as she cringed in Emma's jumpers that were too loose, too big for her. Then, as if lost in the cold, his sister hibernated, slept and slept through the nights and large parts of the days. So that Emma began to say, she must be ill, there must be something wrong with her, some disease, why does she sleep so much Yassir, why?

15

Possessive of Manaal, he had shrugged, Aberdeen's fresh air, and not explained that his sister had always been like that, easily tired, that she reacted to life's confusions by digging herself into sleep.

When they left the airport behind them and began to pass Riyadh, Manaal suddenly said that to make sure they get to the right house, she had better drop in on her friend Zahra. Zahra's mother, a Bulgarian, was a good friend of Mrs K and they would know where the house was.

'I thought you knew where it is?'

'I do – but it's better to be sure. It's on our way anyway.'

'Isn't it too early to go banging on people's doors?'

'No, it's nearly five. Anyway her parents are away – they've gone to Hajj.'

'Who? The Bulgarian woman? You're joking.'

'No, *wallahi*,' Manaal seemed amused by his surprise. 'Zahra's mother prays and fasts Ramadan. We were teasing her the last time I went there, telling her that when she comes back from Hajj, she'll start covering her hair and wearing long sleeves. And she said, "No never, your country is too hot; it's an oven." ' Manaal did an impersonation of grammatically incorrect Arabic with a Bulgarian accent which made Yassir laugh. He thought of Zahra's father, a man who was able to draw his foreign wife to Islam, and Yassir attributed to him qualities of strength and confidence.

The house, in front of which Manaal told him to stop, had a high wall around it. The tops of the trees, that grew inside, fell over the wall shading the pavement. Manaal banged on the metal door – there was no bell. She banged with her palms, and peered through the chink in the door to see if anyone was coming.

Yassir opened the car door to let in some air but there was hardly any breeze. There were tears in the plastic of Manaal's seat from which bits of yellow foam protruded. There was a crack in the window, fine and long, like a map of the Nile and one of the doors in the back was stuck and could never be opened. This car, he thought, would not pass its MOT in Aberdeen; it would not be deemed Road Worthy. What keeps it going here is *baraka*.

The car had seen finer days in his father's lifetime. Then it was solid and tinged with prestige. Now more than anything else, its decay was proof of the passing away of time, the years of Yassir's absence. He had suggested to his mother and Manaal that he should buy them a new one. Indeed this had been one of the topics of his stay – A new car – The house needs fixing – Parts of the garden wall are crumbling away – Why don't you get out of this dump and move to a new house? But his mother and sister tended to put up with things. Like with Manaal recently losing her job. She had worked since graduation with a Danish aid agency, writing reports in their main office in Souk Two. When they had reduced their operations in the South, staff cuts followed. 'Start looking for a new job,' he told her, 'or have you got certain plans that I don't know of yet?' She laughed and said, 'When you leave I'll start looking for a job and no, there are no certain plans. There is no one on the horizon yet.'

It was a joke between them. There is no one on the horizon yet. She wrote this at the bottom of letters, letters in Arabic that Emma could not read. Year after year. She was twenty-six now and he could feel the words touched by the frizzle of anxiety. 'Every university graduate is abroad, making money so that he can come back and marry a pretty girl like you,' he had said recently to her. 'Really?' she replied with a sarcasm that was not characteristic of her.

From the door of Zahra's house, Manaal looked at Yassir in the car and shrugged, then banged again with both hands. But she must have heard someone coming for she raised her hand to him and nodded.

The girl who opened the door had a towel wrapped around her hair like a turban. She kissed Manaal and he could hear, amidst their greetings, the words shower and sorry. They walked towards him, something he was not expecting and before he could get out of the car the girl leaned, and through the open window of the seat next to his, extended her hand. The car filled up with the smell of soap and shampoo, he thought his hand would later smell of her soap. She had the same colouring as his daughter Samia, the froth of cappuccino, dark-grey eyes, thick eyebrows. Her face was dotted with pink spots, round and raised like little sweets. He imagined those grey eyes soft with sadness when she examined her acne in the bathroom mirror, running her fingertips over the bumps.

With a twig and some pebbles, Zahra drew them a map of the painter's house in the dust of the pavement. She sat on her heels rather primly, careful not to get dust on her jellabia. She marked the main road and where they should turn left. When you see a house with no garden walls, no fence, she said, that's where you should turn left.

She stood up, dusted off her hands and when Manaal got into the car, she waved to them until they turned and were out of sight. Yassir drove back on to the main road, from the dust to the asphalt. The asphalt road was raised and because it had no pavements, its sides were continually being eroded, eaten away. They looked jagged, crumbly. The afternoon was beginning to mellow; sunset was drawing near.

'I imagine that when Samia grows up she will look like your friend,' he said.

'Maybe, yes. I haven't thought of it before,' Manaal said. 'Did you like the earrings for Samia?'

He nodded. His mother had given him a pair of earrings for Samia. He had thanked her and not said that his daughter's ears were not pierced.

'She's beginning to accept the situation.' His voice had a tinge of bravado about it. He was talking about his mother and Manaal knew. She was looking out of the window. She turned to him and said, 'She likes the photographs that you send. She shows them to everyone.'

Yassir had been sending photographs from Aberdeen. Photographs of Emma and Samia. Some were in the snow, some taken in the Winter Gardens at Duthie Park, some at home.

'So why doesn't she tell me that? Instead of "What's her name?" or whatever she keeps saying?'

'You should have given her some idea very early on, you should have . . . consulted her,' Manaal spoke slowly, with caution, like she was afraid or just tired.

'And what would she have said if I had asked her? Tell me, what do you think she would have said?'

'I don't know.'

'You do know.'

'How can I?'

'She would have said no and then what?'

'I don't know. I just know that it was wrong to suddenly write a letter and say "I got married" – in the past tense. Nobody does that.'

He didn't answer her. He did not like the hurt in her voice, like it was her own hurt not their mother's.

As if his silence disturbed her and she wanted the conversation to continue she said, 'It wasn't kind.'

'It was honest.'

'But it was hard. She was like someone ill when she read your letter. Defeated and ill . . .'

'She'll come to accept it.'

'Of course she'll come to accept it. That's the whole point. It's inevitable but you could have made it easier for her, that's all.' Then in a lighter tone she said, 'Do something theatrical. Get down on your knees and beg for her forgiveness.'

They laughed at this together, somewhat deliberately to ease the tension. What he wanted to do was explain, speak about Emma and say, She welcomed me, I was on the periphery and she let me in. Do people get tortured to death in that dentist's chair or was I going to be the first? he had asked Emma that day, and made her smile, when he stumbled out of pain and spoke to her with lips numb with procaine.

'It would have been good if Emma and Samia had come with you,' Manaal was saying.

'I wanted that too.'

'Why didn't they?' She had asked that question before as had others. He gave different reasons to different people. Now in the car he felt that Manaal was asking deliberately, wanting him to tell her the truth. Could he say that from this part of the world Emma wanted malleable pieces, not the random whole? She desired frankincense from the Body Shop, tahina safe in a supermarket container.

'She has fears,' he said.

'What fears?'

'I don't know. The sandfly, malaria . . . Some rubbish like that.' He felt embarrassed and disloyal.

They heard the sunset azan when they began to look for the house without a garden wall which Zahra had told them about. But there were many houses like that, people built their homes and ran out of money by the time it came to build the garden wall. So they turned left off the asphalt road anyway when they reached El-Ma'moura, hoping that Manaal would be able to recognise the street or the house.

'Nothing looks familiar to you?' he asked.

'But everything looks different than the last time I was here,' she said. 'All those new houses, it's confusing.'

There were no roads, just tracks made by previous cars, hardly any pavements. They drove through dust and stones. The houses in various stages of construction stood in straight lines. In some parts the houses formed a square around an large empty area, as if marking a place which would always be empty, where houses would not be allowed to be built.

'Maybe it's this house,' Manaal said. He parked, they rang the bell but it was the wrong house.

Back in the car they drove through the different tracks and decided to ask around. How many foreigners were living in this area anyway? People were bound to know them.

Yassir asked a man sitting in front of his house, one knee against his chest, picking his toenails. Near him an elderly man was praying, using a newspaper as a mat. The man didn't seem to know but he gave Yassir several elaborate suggestions.

Yassir asked some people who were walking past but again they didn't know. This was taking a long time as everyone he asked seemed willing to engage him in conversation.

'It's your turn,' he said to Manaal when they saw a woman coming out of her house.

She went towards the woman and stood talking to her. Sunset was nearly over by then, the western sky, the houses, the dusty roads were all one colour, like the flare that burns off the rig, he thought. Manaal stood, a dark silhouette against red and brick. One hand reached out to hold her hair from blowing and her thin elbows made an angle with her head and neck from which the light came through. This is what I would paint, Yassir thought, if I knew how, I would paint Manaal like this, with her elbows sticking out against the setting sun.

When she came back she seemed pleased, 'We're nearly there,' she said, 'that woman knew them. First right, and it's the second house.'

As soon as they turned right, Manaal recognised the one-storey house with the blue gate. She got out before him and rang the bell.

*   *   *

Ronan K. was older than Yassir had imagined. He looked like a football coach, overweight yet light in his movements. The light from the lamp near the gate made him look slightly bald. He recognised Manaal, and as they stepped into a large bare courtyard while he closed the gate behind them, she launched into a long explanation of why they had come and how they had nearly got lost on the way.

The house inside had no tiles on the floors, its surface was of uneven textured stone, giving it the appearance that it was unfinished, still in the process of being built. Yet the furniture was arranged in an orderly way, and there were carpets on the floor. Birds rustled in a cage near the kitchen door. On one of the walls there was a painting of the back of a woman in a *tobe*, balancing a basket on her head.

'One of yours?' Yassir asked but Ronan said no, he did not like to hang his own paintings in the house.

'All my work is on the roof,' he said and from the kitchen he got a tray with a plastic jug full of *kerkadeh* and ice and three glasses. Some of the ice splashed into the glasses as he began to pour, and a pool of redness gathered in the tray, sliding slowly around in large patterns.

'You have a room on the roof?' Yassir asked.

'That's where I paint,' Ronan said. 'I lock it though, we've had many *haramiah* in the area. Not that they would steal my paintings but it's better to be careful. I'm in there most nights though, the *kahrabah* permitting.'

Hearing the Arabic words for thieves and electricity made Yassir smile. He remembered Manaal copying the way Zahra's mother spoke. He wondered how well Ronan K. knew Arabic.

'My wife has the key. But she is right next door. The neighbours' daughter had a baby last week. There's a party of some kind there,' and he looked at Manaal as if for an explanation.

'A *simayah*,' she said.

'That's right,' said Ronan, 'a *simayah*. Maybe you could you go over and get the key from her? It's right next door.'

'Is it Amna and her people?' Manaal asked him. 'I've seen them here before.'

'Yes, that's them.'

'Last time I was here, Amna walked in with chickens to put in your freezer. There wasn't enough room in theirs.'

'Chickens with their heads still on them and all the insides,' said Ronan, 'Terrible . . . This morning she brought over a leg of lamb,' and he gestured vaguely towards the kitchen.

'So who had the baby?' Manaal asked.

'Let's see if I can get this one right,' he said. 'The sister of Amna's husband, who happens to be – just to get things complicated – married to the cousin of Amna's mother.'

They laughed because Ronan gave an exaggerated sigh as if he had done a lot of hard work.

'I thought you said it was the neighbours' daughter,' said Yassir.

'Well this Amna character,' he said and Manaal laughed and nodded at the word 'character', 'she is living with her in-laws, so it is really the in-laws, house.'

Manaal got up to go and Ronan said, 'I'll tell you what. Just throw the keys up to us on the roof. We'll wait for you there. It will save time.'

The roof was dark and cool, its floor more uneven than that of the house had been. The ledge all around it was low, only knee-high. El-Ma'moura lay spread out before them, the half-built houses surrounded by scaffolding, the piles of sand and discarded bricks. Shadows of stray dogs made their way through the rubble. Domes of cardboard marked the places where the caretakers of the houses and their families lived. Their job was to guard the bags of cement, the toilets, the tiles that came for the new houses. Once the houses were built they would linger, drawing water from the pipes that splashed on the embryonic streets, until they were eventually sent away.

From the house next door came the sounds of children playing football, scuffling, names called out loud. A woman's voice shrieked from indoors. Yassir and Ronan sat on the ledge. He offered Yassir a cigarette and Yassir accepted though he hadn't smoked for several years. Ronan put his box of matches between them. It had a picture of a crocodile on it, mouth wide open, tail arched up in the air. Yassir had forgotten how good it felt to strike a match, flick grey ash away. It was one of the things he and Emma had done together – given up smoking.

'A long way from Aberdeen, or rather Aberdeen is a long way from here,' Ronan said.

'Have you been there before?'

'I know it well, my mother originally came from Elgin. They can be a bit parochial up there, don't you think?'

At the back of Yassir's mind questions formed themselves, rose out of a sense of habit, but dropped languidly as if there was no fuel to vocalise them. What was this man doing here, in a place where even the nights were hot and alcohol was forbidden? Where there was little comfort and little material gain? The painter sat on his roof and like the raised spots on the girl's face did not arouse in Yassir derision, only passive wonder.

'If you look this way,' Ronan said, 'you can see the airport – where the red and blue lights are. Sometimes I see the aeroplanes circling and landing. They pass right over me when they take off. I see the fat bellies of planes full of people going away.

Last August we had so much rain. This whole area was flooded – we couldn't drive to the main road. The Nile rose and I could see it with my telescope – even though it is far from here.'

'How long have you been here?' Yassir asked.

'Fifteen years.'

'That's a long time.'

Giant wisps of white brushed the sky as if the smoke from their cigarettes had risen high, expanded and stood still. Stars were pushing their way into view, gathering around them the darkest dregs of night. On the roof, speaking Emma's language for the first time in two weeks, Yassir missed her, not with the light eagerness he had known on the rigs but with something else, something plain and unwanted: the grim awareness of distance. He knew why he had wanted her to come with him, not to 'see', but so that Africa would move her, startle her, touch her in some irreversible way.

Manaal threw up the keys, Ronan opened the locked room and put the light on. It was a single bulb which dangled from the ceiling, speckled with the still bodies of black insects. The room smelt of paint, a large fan stood in the corner. Conscious of his ignorance, Yassir was silent as Ronan, cigarette drooping from his mouth, showed him one painting after the other. 'I like them,' he said and it was true. They were clear and uncluttered, the colours light, giving an impression of sunlight. Most were of village scenes, mud houses, one of children playing with a goat, one of a tree that had fallen into the river.

'Paper is my biggest problem,' said Ronan. 'The brushes and paints last for quite some time. But if I know someone who is going abroad I always ask them for paper.'

'Is it special paper that you need?'

'Yes, thicker for water colours.'

'I like the one of the donkey in front of the mud house,' said Yassir.

'The Hilton don't seem to want mud houses.'

'Did they tell you that?'

'No, I just got this feeling.'

'That means I could get them at a discount?'

'Maybe . . . How many were you thinking of taking?'

Yassir choose three, one of them the children with the goat because he thought Samia might like that. He paid after some haggling. Downstairs the birds were asleep in their cage, there was no longer any ice in the jug of *kerkadeh*. Manaal was waiting for him by the gate. She had a handful of dates from next door which she offered to Ronan and Yassir. The dates were dry and cracked uncomfortably under Yassir's teeth before softening into sweetness. It was now time to leave. He shook hands with Ronan. The visit was a success; he had achieved what he came for.

Manaal slept in the car on the way home. Yassir drove through streets busier than the ones he had found in the afternoon. This was his last day in Khartoum. Tomorrow night a plane would take him to Paris, another plane to Glasgow then the train to Aberdeen. Perhaps Ronan K. would be on his roof tomorrow night, watching Air France rise up over the new houses of El-Ma'moura.

The city was acknowledging his departure, recognising his need for a farewell. Headlamps of cars jerked in the badly lit streets, thin people in white floated like clouds. Voices, rumbling lorries, trucks leaning to one side snorting fumes. On a junction with a busier road, a small bus went past carrying a wedding party. It was lit inside, an orange light that caught the singing faces, the clapping hands. Ululations, the sound of a drum, lines from a song. Yassir drove on and gathered around him what he would take back with him, the things he could not deliver. Not the beads, not the paintings, but other things. Things devoid of the sense of their own worth. Manaal's silhouette against the rig's flare, against a sky dyed with *kerkadeh*. The scent of soap and shampoo in his car, a man picking his toenails, a page from a newspaper spread out as a mat. A voice that said, I see the planes circling at night, I see their lights . . . all the people going away. Manaal saying, you could have made it easier for her, you could have been more kind.

Visitors

The queue had already reached the gate by the time Amina arrived. Patients and parents squatting on the ground, waiting for her and the other two doctors to arrive. It was Tuesday – the one day in the week when the out-patient clinic was held at the Cheshire Home. All the patients were children; some were resident at the home but the majority had made long journeys across Khartoum.

Amina parked her car near the door, under the sign that said Cheshire Home in Arabic and in English. It was January and she felt invigorated by the cool fresh breeze; it was rare when the sun ceased its merciless assault. She wore a black cardigan which had a slimming effect on her plump figure. Everything about her was large and healthy, her nose, her mouth, her speech, and she was young, still training in orthopedics. Tuesday was her favorite day of the week as the work was light compared to the gruelling days at the hospital. It was also a treat to drive to the Cheshire Home, situated as it was in one of the most elegant parts of the city. All the houses were built during the colonial period for the new University's staff: spacious bungalows with large leafy gardens. Gravel stones marked the curves of the driveways, thick hedges separated each house from the next.

The heels of her sandals crunched the stones as she walked past the people in the queue. The desert winter had powdered their arms grey with chapped skin. A harsh sun had faded away the colour from the clothes they wore. They stirred now as she approached, relieved that their ordeal was nearly over. She felt pleased at the effect she was having, she enjoyed making an entrance. An elderly thin man, got up and clutching his son's shoulder greeted her.

'You are Hassan's father? I was asking about you last week because I think Hassan might be able to go home now. Are you taking him today? I could give you a lift if you wait for me until the clinic is over,' she spoke quickly not waiting for his answer and all the time swinging his son's hand in hers. Hassan was six years old, beautiful with liquid golden eyes and soft dusty hair. She was in love with him, in the simple way that young women who have not yet had children sometimes feel.

'Did you eat breakfast, Hassan?' she asked. She always asked him that question because she liked the way he answered.

'*Alhamdu-lilah*,' he lisped. He never said 'Yes, *Alhamdu-lilah*' as other would do. He always omitted the 'yes', so that she was always left not knowing whether he had eaten or not.

Today, as she walked into the door of the Home, she wondered how the father could be so old and battered.

'Sakeenah,' she called inside, 'don't you have any Vaseline for Hassan? His face and arms are all dry and cracked.' Sakeenah looked after the children in the Home. She lived there and only went home on the weekends. Sakeenah thought Hassan was special. Serene, unlike other children. When the Qur'an was recited on the radio, she told Amina, Hassan would leave his play and listen intently. Amina was inclined to be more cynical and believed that Hassan's charm lay in his failure to comprehend fully his disability. He was still too young. Not like the older children, those who were resentful and hurt, who understood that when they grew up they would not drive a bus, would not make desirable brides.

In between seeing patients, the doctors drank tea and talked to each other. 'You won't be putting so much sugar in your tea Dr Musa now that there is going to be rationing and coupons,' Amina teased, as the senior doctor added a third spoon to his small cup.

'Three isn't much,' he answered shaking his head and dropping cigarette ash on the linoleum, 'and anyway these new regulations are ridiculous, they will prove to be impractical to implement and will soon be dropped.'

'But I think the government is serious this time,' said Dr Fareed, 'they don't have enough money to import all the sugar the country needs. It might be difficult to ration consumption outside the capital but not within Khartoum.'

There was no time for Dr Musa to argue because Hassan and his father came in and the three doctors began to examine the boy's wasted left leg. It was paralysed from the waist down, the result of polio which he had contracted at the age of two. They all agreed that the new calipers were suitable and that he need not remain resident at the Cheshire House any longer.

Amina drove Hassan and his father home, both of them sitting at the back. They lived in one of a group of mud houses at the outskirts of the city. She had to drive across the new bridge, turn right into a good asphalt road with lorries thundering into the capital from the villages further south. Along the banks of the Nile were villas with spacious gardens. Amina once had a school friend who lived in one of those villas. There was a swimming pool inside with eucalyptus leaves floating on top of the water.

Hassan's home was directly across from the villas. She had to leave the asphalt road, drive down onto the sand. The children playing in the dirt looked up at the approaching car. They were a mixture of ages. Girls in torn dresses that slid off their shoulders,

boys in faded T-shirts that hovered above their navels. They left
their toys, the tin cans they were rolling with sticks and the
rejected car tyres they had been pushing, and crowded around the
car that now parked in front of Hassan's house.

'Do come in, Doctor, you are welcome, do come in!' the father
insisted as he struggled with the door lock.

'Not today, Hajj, thank you but I can't today,' said Amina
twisting in her seat to unlock the door for them. 'Insha Allah, I will
come one day when I have more time.'

'When? When will you come? On Friday?'

'I don't know now, but Insha Allah I will come sometime next
week. Goodbye Hassan!' and although the old man had not closed
the car door properly she was off, a cloud of dust after her.

Amina kept her promise a week later, laden with gifts for Hassan and
his family. The gifts were clothes which she knew they needed and,
on a sudden impulse, half her month's salary to give to the mother.
She found the mud house easily enough, entered first a small
courtyard, the floor sand like outside. A dripping tap a foot off
the floor, a *zeer*, the walls of the house at close range were a dark
reddish brown with flecks of yellow straw. Amina had to stoop a little
underneath the doorway. It was easy to see where Hassan had got his
good looks. His mother Zeinab was slim, tall and straight. She had
smooth skin and youthful rounded features. Child number five a girl,
clung to her, nursing at her breast. The girl was three years old but
she looked younger. Her hair defied gravity, it stood up straight,
coarse and strong, with the soft light in the room filtering through it.

'If I had known you were coming I would have bathed the
children.' Zeinab was flustered, she walked about the small room
shooing the children out. She straightened the sheet on the bed
that Amina sat on and seemed glad that it was clean. The plastic
bags that Amina had dropped carelessly near her on the bed bulged
with promise but there was no time to think of that. Furtively,

secretly, lest Amina noticed and raised a polite objection, Zeinab gave her eldest daughter money to buy the visitor a drink from the canteen store half a mile away.

The room that Amina sat in was the only room in the house. It was dark, the ceiling was low, and there was one small window which revealed a similar house an arm's length away. In the room, there were three beds set up against each wall and in the corner, looking out of place, was a glass cabinet. In it Zeinab carefully kept her glasses, plates and trays.

When the daughter came back with the Pepsi bottle, Zeinab placed a small metal table in front of Amina. She took out a tray from the glass cabinet, a clean glass. She pushed the children, who were pressed against the doorway, out of the way and squatted to wash the glass once more under the tap. Still carrying the child, she placed the tray, glass and bottle on the table before Amina. They swayed precariously. The fixed look of the children in the doorway was held by the cool bottle covered with drops of condensation.

Rumour had spread among the neighbours of the visitor, and soon the room was full of curious women. Enjoying being the centre of attention, Amina was soon in her element, chatting about the sugar shortage, writing prescriptions, examining children. To the women's amusement, she launched into a lecture on the merits of the contraceptive coil. She wrote letters for some women addressed to their relatives who lived in villages outside Khartoum. They dictated the words to her and she wrote them on bits of lined paper that she found in her handbag. Most of the families including Hassan's were part of the recent rise in urban migration and their ties to their home villages were still strong. As Amina got up to go, Zeinab told her that they would visit her one day and insisted that she draw a map of her house for them.

Weeks later, with the youngest child in her arms and Hassan struggling behind, Zeinab did return the visit. Amina, who had forgotten them, was surprised to see them. She was taken aback, because she had not really expected them to come. She avoided her father's enquiring eyes and seated them outside on the verandah. A look at her watch showed her that she only had half an hour before her fiancé and his mother arrived. If they saw the ragged Zeinab, there would be a lot of questions she did not want to answer.

Perhaps they had come begging, she thought with sudden cynicism. She had been kind to them once and they were going to take advantage of that. Self-righteous anger swelled up in her and she surrendered to it. But they did not look like they had come to beg. Zeinab's feet were squeezed into a pair of slippers that were obviously not hers, too small, borrowed from a friend or a neighbour. A pink plastic flower decorated each slipper, garish, now caked with sand. And how sweet Hassan looked in the new clothes she had bought him! He was bathed and his hair brushed hard over his head so that it was nearly straight. But he looked thinner than he had been at the Home. 'They feed them well at Cheshire's,' thought Amina. 'Better than the food that they get in their own homes.' He was telling her how he could not go to school with his brothers and sisters because there was a trench on the way which he could not jump over. But Amina was not listening.

'I will go indoors, get them a drink and then quickly offer to drive them home,' she thought.

Their visit was an encroachment on her life. She had wanted them to be distant, passive. She would visit them whenever the whim to be generous overtook her. She would be the one who would be in control of the relationship. She did not want them here, prim and formal, out of place in her own world.

'Take this with you inside,' said Zeinab as Amina got up. 'It is something for you; empty the pail and bring it back.' She lifted a blue plastic pail with a white cover from the floor next to her and handed it to Amina.

'Thank you, Zeinab, you needn't have got me anything,' said Amina exasperated now and trying not to show it. So was it friendship that Zeinab was after, bringing her a gift like Amina had done a few weeks ago? Amina carried the pail warily and wished she had never visited them in the first place. What could be inside the pail? Probably greasy pastries cooked in the least hygienic of places. She shuddered and thought that she would have to throw them away. It was a waste but she knew that nobody in her family would eat them. And although time was tight, the pail would have to be washed before she gave it back to Zeinab. Amina sighed as she walked into the kitchen and opened the fridge to remove two Pepsi bottles.

On the kitchen table she placed the pail, lifted its cover and looked inside. But instead of Zeinab's home-made food that she dreaded, there were pounds and pounds of that elusive white substance every household in Khartoum craved: sugar.

The Ostrich

'Y ou look like something from the Third World,' he said and I
let myself feel hurt, glancing downwards so that he would
not see the look in my eyes. I didn't answer his taunting smile like
he expected me to, didn't say, 'And where do *you* come from?' I let
him put his arm around me by way of greeting and gave him the
trolley with my suitcases to push.

He must have seen me first, I thought, while I was scanning the
faces of the people who were waiting at the terminal, he must have
been watching me all the time. And I suddenly felt ashamed not
only for myself but for everyone else who arrived with me on that
aeroplane. Our shabby luggage, our stammering in front of the
immigration officer, our clothes that seemed natural a few hours
back, now crumpled and out of place.

So I didn't tell him about the baby, though I imagined I would
tell him right away in the airport as soon as we met. Nor did I
confess that at times I longed not to return, that in Khartoum I felt
everything was real and our life in London a hibernation.

I had to remember to walk next to him not loiter behind. I was
reluctant to leave the other passengers. A few hours ago we were a
cohesive unit, smug and loud at Khartoum airport, the lucky few
heading north. In the aeroplane we ate the same food, faced the

same direction and acknowledged each other with nods and small smiles. Now we were to separate, dazzled by the bright lights of the terminal, made humble by the plush carpeted floors, chastened by the perfect announcements one after the other, words we could understand, meanings we could not. From the vacuum of the terminal where all sound was absorbed we would disperse into the cloudy city and soon forget the pride with which we bought our tickets and left our home. He dislikes it if I walk a few steps behind him, what would people think, he says, that we are backward, barbaric. He sneers at the Arab women in black *abayas* walking behind their men. Oppressed, that's what people would think of them. Here they respect women, treat them as equal; we must be the same he says. So I have to be careful not to fall behind him in step and must bear the weight of his arm around my shoulder, another gesture he had decided to imitate to prove that though we are Arabs and Africans, we can be modern too.

We waited outside the terminal for the Air Bus to arrive. Only two months away and I had forgotten how wet this country could be. Already my painted toes stuck out of my soaked sandals, a mockery. He looked well, he told me his research was progressing, he had been to Bath for a conference where his supervisor read a paper. 'It had an acknowledgement of me at the bottom of the first page,' he said, 'because I did the simulation work on the computer. In italics, the author thanks Majdy El-Shaykh and so on.'

Majdy will write his own papers one day, he will complete his Ph.D. and have Dr before his name. His early doubts, his fears of failure are receding away. I should have felt proud. I supposed I would one day, but at the moment I felt tired and insincere. I strained to feel the baby move inside me, but there was only silence.

'You are envied Sumra,' my mother said, 'envied for living abroad where it is so much more comfortable than here. Don't complain, don't be ungrateful.' But when she saw the resentment on my face she softened and said, 'It will be easier when you have the baby. Something to fill your day, you won't have time to be homesick then.' Yet I imagined that I could just not come back, slip into my old life, month after month and he would forget me in time, send me my divorce paper as an afterthought, marry someone else perhaps. He would marry an English woman with yellow hair and blue eyes. I catch him thinking that sometimes, if he had waited a little, not rushed into this marriage, he could have married a woman like the ones he admires on TV. We married so that he would not bring back a foreign wife with him like so many Sudanese students did or, worse, marry her and never come back. Who wants to go back to the Sudan after tasting the good life of the West? With a Sudanese wife though he would surely come back. This is what his family told me, half in jest, half in earnest. So I was flattered with presents, a big wedding, a good-looking educated bridegroom and the chance to go abroad. No reason for me to refuse. But perhaps they cannot twist fate; perhaps I am not strong enough to hold him to his roots.

If I find a way to live here forever, he says, if only I could get a work permit. I can't imagine I could go back, back to the petrol queue, computers that don't have electricity to work on or paper to print on. Teach dim-witted students who never held a calculator in their hands before. And a salary, a monthly salary that is less than what an unemployed person gets here in a week! Calculate it if you don't believe me.

He had answers to all the objections I raised. Morality, what morality do we have when our politicians are corrupt, when we buy arms to fuel a civil war instead of feeding the hungry? And don't talk of racism! We are more racist than the British, how have we Northerners always treated the Southern Sudanese?

The bus came at last and we sat upstairs while the green countryside around Heathrow drifted past. The green leaves in

Khartoum are a different green, sharper, drier, arrogant in the desert heat. I know this bus, I know this route: it is as familiar as a film one sees several times. Two years in London and when I come back after two months in Khartoum I feel like I am starting all over again. Two months wiped out two years, and I am a stranger once again.

'Did you meet anyone on the plane that you knew?' Majdy asked. One always does travelling to and from Khartoum, a small city with many familiar faces. I lied and said no. I lied and did not tell him that, on the first part of the journey from Khartoum to Cairo, I met the Ostrich.

I never could train myself to remember his real name. I always thought of him as the Ostrich and maybe I even called him that to his face, although I have no memory of his response. More likely I told my friends and was probably disappointed that they didn't start using that name too.

He really did look like an ostrich with his thin protruding neck and his long dangling arms. He walked head craned forward, raised eyebrows, wide tentative steps. His hair was light in colour, sticking out in a large Afro that swayed when he moved, matted flat at the back of his head as if he was too lazy to reach that far with his comb. It was when we were in our second year at University that he descended upon our class, after we had sorted ourselves out into groups, after we had set labels on each other. He should have been in his fourth year, but he lost two years when a speeding car knocked him down. His body healed, but his eyes were permanently damaged and they remained large, bleary and unfocused. They placed him in a world, which he alone inhabited, where everything was fuzzy and everyone saw him as unclearly as he saw them.

'Your bags were so heavy,' Majdy was saying 'Did you have to pay excess?'

'No . . . It's the grapefruit I got you and the white plaited cheese that you like.'

'From the land of famine you bring me food.' Again the mocking tone, but I knew he was pleased. They were things he secretly missed.

'It's not as bad as they make it out to be here on TV or not in Khartoum anyway. Normal, I suppose, weddings, funerals, but still a feeling of depression. Everything is so expensive . . . and everyone wants to leave. Every family I visited has someone abroad. In the Gulf, in Egypt, in America. Remember your neighbours Ali and Samir?'

'The ones with the white Mercedes.'

'Mercedes or not they're away too. Ali in Bahrain and Samir in Norway. Imagine Norway, and his sister and her husband are busy filling in forms to immigrate to Australia.' I laughed. The brain drain was like a scramble.

'That's what I keep telling you. There's no future back there and if people who were much better off than us aren't coping, how can we ever cope if we go back? I'm doing the right thing, sticking it out here in any way that I can.'

The Ostrich had a brother who worked in the Gulf. He sent him a watch that could beep. I remember the Ostrich bringing it up to his nose twisting his face sideways so that he could peer at the time. It was a novelty for most of us, the first digital watch that we ever saw. The alarm would go off at the end of the lecture, a reminder to the teacher to end the class. We would giggle then, us girls sitting in the front row. We always had the front rows. We would reserve the seats in advance, throwing our copybooks on the desk, throwing extra copybooks for our friends. There were hundreds of us in one class and we would sit on the painful wooden seats. Numb behinds, arms brushing arms, knees against knees. And I remember the girls who would come in late, their footsteps loud in the hushed room, walking up a few steps and slipping in beside their friends. The Ostrich always floated in late and sat at the back where the blackboard was out of focus and he could not take down any notes, where he poked pencils in his hair, his ears, his nose and waited for his watch to go beep. It never occurred to us to offer him a seat in front.

He never inspired the self-conscious concern reserved for the handicapped. We did not compete to offer him help and I remember him once telling me that I looked nice in blue and I had laughed and asked him how he could tell or that he would say the same thing to a donkey given the chance. I was cruel to him. Sometimes I looked into his eyes and they were beautiful, amber and mysterious like a newborn child's. Welcoming, like nests of whirling honey. Sometimes I felt sickened by their bleariness; the long eyelashes caked with sleep.

I had forgotten how small the flat was, how thin the walls were. Student accommodation. The cleanliness comes as a surprise, this clean land free of dust and insects. Everywhere carpet and everything compact like boxes inside boxes, the houses stuck together defensively. September and it is already winter, already cold. The window, how many hours did I spend looking out of this window? For two years I looked out at strangers, unable to make stories about them, unable to tell who was rich who was poor, who mended pipes and who healed the ill. And sometimes (this was particularly disturbing) not even knowing who was a man and who was a woman. Strangers I must respect, strangers who were better than me. This is what Majdy says. Every one of them is better than us. See the man who is collecting the rubbish, he is not ravaged by malaria, anaemia, bilharzia, he can read the newspaper, write a letter, he has a television in his house and his children go to a school where they get taught from glossy books. And if they are clever, if they show a talent in music or science they will be encouraged and they might be important people one day. I look at the man who collects the rubbish and I am ashamed that he picks bags with our filth in them. When I pass him on the road I avert my eyes.

And now that I am back, the room rises up to strangle me. The window beckons and it is already dark outside. I was wrong to return. All the laughter and confidence has been left behind. What am I doing here? A stranger suddenly appearing on the stage with no part to play, no lines to read. Majdy points out the graffiti for me, look, 'Black Bastards' on the wall of the mosque, 'Paki go home' on the newsagent's door, do you know what it means, who wrote it? I breed a new fear of not knowing, never knowing who these enemies are. How would I recognise them while they can so easily recognise me? The woman who sells me stamps (she is old, I must respect her age), the librarian who could not spell my name while the queue behind me grew (I will be reading her books for free), or the bus driver I angered by not giving him the correct change (it's my fault, I must obey the sign on the door). Which one of them agrees with what's written on the walls?

There are others, Majdy's new friends, so and so is good he says, friendly. He invites them here, men with kind eyes and women who like the food I cook. But I must be wary; there are things I mustn't say when they are here. I mentioned polygamy once saying we shouldn't condemn something that Allah had permitted, remarking that Majdy's father had a second wife. When they left he slapped me, and fool that I was I didn't understand what I had done wrong. Why, why I asked and he slapped me more. It's worse when you don't understand, he said; at least have a feeling that you have said something wrong. They can forgive you for your ugly colour, your thick lips and rough hair, but you must think modern thoughts, be like them in the inside if you can't be from the outside. And what stuck in my mind after the stinging ebbed away, after the apologetic caresses, what clung to me and burned me time and time again, were his comments about how I looked. I would stand in front of the mirror and, Allah forgive me, hate my face.

You look beautiful in blue the Ostrich said and when I was cruel he said, but I can be a judge of voices can I not? I didn't ask him what he thought of my voice, I walked away. It must have been in the evening that I was wearing blue. It was white tobes in the morning, coloured ones for the evening. The evening lectures were special, leisurely; there was time after lunch to shower, to have a nap. To walk from the hostels in groups and pairs, past the young boy selling peanuts, past the closed post office, past the *neem* trees with the broken benches underneath. Jangly earrings, teeth snapping chewing gum and kohl in our eyes. The tobes slipping off our carefully combed hair, lifting our hands putting them back on again. Tightening the material, holding it under our left arm. I miss these gestures already left behind. (Majdy says: if you cover your hair in London they'll think I was forcing you to do that. They won't believe it is what you want.) So I must walk unclothed, imagining cotton on my hair, lifting my hand to adjust an imaginary tobe.

The sunset prayers were a break in the middle of these evening lectures. One communist lecturer keen to assert his atheism ignored the rustling of the notebooks, the shuffling of restless feet, the screech of the Ostrich's alarm. Only when someone called out, 'A break for the prayers!', did he stop teaching. I will always see the grass, patches of dry yellow, the rugs of palm-fibre laid out. They curl at the edges and when I put my forehead on the ground I can smell the grass underneath. Now that we have a break we must hurry, for it is as if the birds have heard the azan and started to pray before us. I can hear their praises, see the branches bow down low to receive them as they dart to the tree. Feel their urgency, they know how quickly the sun slips away and then it will be too late. We wash from a corner tap taking turns. The Ostrich squats and puts his whole head under the tap, shakes it backwards and drops of water balance on top of his hair. I borrow a mug from the canteen and I am proud, a little vain that I can wash my hands, face, arms and feet with only one mug. Sandals discarded, we line up and the boy from the canteen joins us, his torn clothes stained with tea. Another lecturer, not finding room on the mat, spreads his handkerchief on the grass. If I was not praying I would stand with my feet crunching the gravel stones and watch the straight lines, the men in front, the colourful tobes behind. I would know that I was part of this harmony that I needed no permission to belong. Here in London the birds pray discreetly and I pray alone. A printed booklet, not a muezzin, tells me the times. Here in London Majdy does not pray. This country, he says, bit by bit chips away at your faith.

There were unwashed dishes in the sink, fragile eggshells to throw away, dirty socks on the floor, on Majdy's desk empty mugs of tea, the twisted cores of apples. I started to tidy up; he switched on the TV. Computer printouts lay on piles on the floor. Many evenings before I went to Khartoum, he would work at his desk while I sat and cut the perforated edges of the sheets, strings of paper with holes. I played with them in my hands, twisting them into shapes, making bracelets and rings like a child. And these were the happy moments of our marriage, when the world outside was forgotten, when his concentration in his work was so intense that he would whistle the tunes of Sudanese songs we knew long ago.

Two months have yielded plenty of computer printouts. When I tidied up, when I unpacked, when he switched off the television and settled at his desk with a mug of tea, a feast awaited me. A feast of the sounds of paper separating from paper, holes settling upon holes, chains of entwined crispness. Now I could sit on the floor with the paper in front of me, lean my back on Majdy's chair and unroll my memories. The Ostrich sitting on the bumper of a car parked inside the University, a number of us around him standing against its windows. Notebooks in our arms, those thin notebooks with a spiral wire holding the pages, a drawing of the University on the front cover. What was the weather like? Hot, very hot – we can smell each other's sweat. Or one of those bright winter days when the sun softens its blows and a breeze whispers around the trees. Dust on the car, inside it; dust clinging to the Ostrich's hair, dust climbing between our toes. The shadows of the tree dance around the Ostrich, elusive patches of shade. What did we speak of in those days, when everything seemed possible and we were naive, believing the University an end not a means? 'Some Emir in the Gulf bought a horse in England for ten million pounds. Imagine ten million in hard currency. It could have built a hospital, schools, roads. Shoes for me, says the Ostrich stretching his feet, his sandals torn, his toes coarse and gnarled, feet that could withstand burning tiles . . . Wish for a coup, the first thing they'll do is close the University, or better still a reason for a strike a month or so before the exams. Postponement and no Fiscal Policy . . . What has that man been going on about all year? Swear I saw last year's paper and couldn't even tell which parts of the lecture notes the answers came from.'

Cinnamon tea, sweet in chipped glasses. Roasted watermelon seeds, the salt dissolving in our mouths, the empty shells falling around like leaves. The Ostrich, a forgotten shell on his lip slides down from the car's bumper, raises his arms, head back and turns around in circles. Under his arms there are patches of wetness, his weak eyes brave the mid-day sun. Laughter bubbles inside him letting loose the shell from his lip. 'The fan,' he says, laughing more, bending forward and slapping his hands together. 'The fan in the common room fell down from the ceiling. You should have seen it. It went whizzing around the room like a top.' We exclaim, we ask questions, no one was hurt, hardly anyone was in the room at the time. He found it funny. Perhaps this is the essence of my country, what I miss most. Those everyday miracles, the poise between normality and chaos. The awe and the breathtaking gratitude for simple things. A place where people say Allah alone is eternal.

*   *   *

I weave paper ribbons with holes, chains; the edges of each sheet are sharp. Grapefruit juice, no one buys for themselves alone, always sharing, competing in generosity (our downfall Majdy says, the downfall of a whole people, a primitive tribal mentality and so inefficient). Pink grapefruit juice, frothy at the top, jagged pieces of ice struck out of large slabs with particles of sand frozen inside. 'Am Ali, the man who makes the juice has to hold down the cover of the mixer. He can make only two glasses at a time, when the electricity fails he can make none. Aubergine sandwiches, the baked plant crushed to a pulp, red hot with pepper, the bread in thin loaves. Bread is rationed now. I stood in a queue for bread every morning in the two months I was back in Khartoum.

Coming across the Ostrich in the library, his nose literally in a large book. Not for him Cost–Benefit Analysis, Rostow's take-off, Pareto's curves. He would be reading poetry from old musty books that perhaps no one looked at except him. He once looked up at me as I passed, his eyes bulging from the strain he was putting them through. He quoted the Andalusian poet Ibn Zaydun,

> *Yes, I have remembered you with longing, at al-Zahra,*
> *when the horizon was bright and the face of the earth gave pleasure,*
> *and the breeze was soft in the late afternoon,*
> *as if it had pity on me.*

I smiled at him then, wondering if he could see my smile, knowing he was memorising the poem.

The Ostrich picked his nose on prime-time television. What he dislodged he rolled leisurely between his thumb and forefinger like a grain of rice. Held it up, peered at it closely narrowing his eyes and then flicked it away. We hooted with laughter as we crowded around the black and white TV set of the girls' hostel, cross-legged on the floor, on each other's laps on wobbling metal chairs, Vaseline glistening on our arms and rollers in our hair. It was a game show, a poetry competition with the flamboyant title, *Knights in the Arena*. When a competitor recites a verse, his opponent must recite one that starts with the last letter of the last word in that verse. The skill was in memory and the ability to throw verses at your opponent, which end with the same letter, depleting his particular stock.

The Ostrich excelled. Leaning back on his chair, his fingers in his nose and in his ears, oblivious to the cameras, to the hundreds who were watching, he gave us the poetry of the pre-Islamic Arabs, their pride in the strength of their tribe. Lovers weeping at the remains of the camp fires from which their beloved had gone away, the Sufi poems of self-annihilation and longing to join the Almighty.

Alienated in his own hazy world, the Ostrich was free. And when he won the prize of fifty pounds (a good amount in those days) and a trophy, he took as many of us as he could to a restaurant by the Nile, where we ate kebabs and watched the moon's reflection flutter in the running water below.

It was late, footsteps no longer sounded in the corridor outside, the heating had gone off and it was cold. I went to get my shawl from the bedroom; it was folded in the cupboard just as I had left it weeks ago. I wrapped it around me and sat cross-legged again on the floor. In the final exams the Ostrich sat next to me in the hall. *Number three*, he whispered, *Number three*, his head on top of his paper, his eyes strangely oscillating. I saw the invigilator look up towards him, towards us. I had helped him before, lending him my notes, nagging him for days to bring them back only to discover he had passed them on to someone else, and in the exams where we always seemed to sit next to each other, whispering a few helpful words here and there whenever I got the chance. That last time though, I peeled my hand off my paper and saw that the ink had been smudged, the paper made thin by my sweat. (Typical inefficiency, Majdy would say, he should have been specially examined, someone reading out the questions to him, noting down his answers.) Shut up, I whispered back, shut up, and when the invigilator walked past I stopped him and complained about the Ostrich. They moved him away, he protested, his eyes darting wildly as if he could not hold them still. He swore, they were harsh and dragged him away. His chair remained overturned next to me until the end of the exam. Why, my friends asked me, why tell on him like that? I graduated, he did not, and for years I did not see him until I met him today on the aeroplane.

But it was not today any more; it was yesterday for the watch on my wrist showed 2 am: midnight London time. I moved the hands slowly, pushing time back. Majdy looked tired from too much concentration. There were shiny dark grooves under his eyes. He picked the pile of printouts from the floor, bald of their edges and began to tidy them up, sort them out into piles. Some he will not want at all; I will use them to line up drawers and give them to the daughter of the Malaysian couple who live on the ground floor. She likes to draw on them.

'I was afraid you wouldn't come back,' Majdy suddenly said. And I wondered if this was the right time so late at night to talk of such things, things that would drive the sleep from our eyes. When I looked at him, he seemed weak and this made him look more beautiful than he had looked at the airport. I remembered the stories his sisters told me about how he was when he first came here. Despairing of ever passing his exams, ever catching up with the work. And now he was nearly through. The rescue package his family sent him has achieved its purpose. 'I work better when you are next to me,' he was saying. 'It is easier to keep awake. When I saw you in the airport today, you brought back many memories to me. Of people I love and I've left behind, of what I once was years ago. I envy you and you find that funny, don't you, but it's true. I envy you because you are displaced yet intact, unchanged while I question everything and I am not sure of anything any more.'

And it was only then, late that night, when he came and sat near me on the floor that I told him about our baby.

That night I dreamt of the Ostrich's bride. She was, like she had told me in the aeroplane, at University with me. In the dream we were in one of the lecture rooms, the fans circling above our head. I made a chain from the perforated edges of the computer paper and gave it to her. She wore it as an ankle bracelet and I was anxious that the paper might tear but she laughed at my fears.

It was the Ostrich who recognised me first in the aeroplane. 'Sumra,' he said, and when I looked blankly at him, my hand luggage in front of me trying to find the way to my seat, 'Don't you remember me, Sumra?' His hair was cut short, his eyes behind dark spectacles and I could tell that he was newly married. From the henna intricately designed on his bride's palms, from the gold bracelets on her arms, the shimmering material of her new tobe, I could tell they were on their honeymoon. We exchanged news the way people do when they have not met for a long time. Is this happiness then, the sudden rush of recognition, the warmth, the shy laughter? Swapping news of others that we mutually knew. Could I have ever believed that the word happiness can be cramped in a few minutes, a few unexpected minutes in the aisle of an aeroplane?

'My brother set up a video shop in Medani, which I run,' the Ostrich said and we both laughed again as if it was something funny, as if we shared a private joke. 'Hindi films are popular,' he rambled in his Ostrich way. 'Nobody understands the language but they keep renting out the films.'

'I remember you from University', she interrupted us. 'I was in my first year when you were in your last.' Her confident smile, her almost flirty manner. I disliked her for making him hide his eyes and cut his hair. And it was uncomfortable trying to remember her face, vaguely familiar though it was, trying to suppress a hurt vanity at the reminder of the disparity in our ages.

Envy is more unwelcome than grief. It took me unaware. Tripped me and I fell into a pool of thoughts that were unreasonable, that should never have been mine. Would she sit on his lap and clean his eyelashes with her manicured hands? Would he write her notes in his large handwriting, the grotesque letters uncontrolled by the lines he couldn't see?

In my seat with the hum of the aircraft in my ears I fought alone my morning sickness and watched the clouds out of the window swirl around. She passed me twice, leaving behind a faint smell of sandalwood, a tinkle of her bracelets, a raised eyebrow, an attractive smile. When the aeroplane landed in Cairo, they said goodbye. No addresses exchanged, no promises made. New passengers boarded and took their place, an Egyptian lady and her daughter who kept writing in a small notebook. And when the aeroplane took off again, I left the Ostrich and Africa behind me as I had done once before.

Today I walked the High Street and looked at the shops. Shelves stacked with food, rows and rows of soft drinks, even the sugar in different types. For these things we had left our home, for these things I was envied. I walked down rows and rows of detergents, of toilet rolls, of frozen meats. People hurried past, time the only thing not in abundance here. I got in the way of others, fiddled with my change at the checkout counter, blocked their way as I tried to read the headlines of newspapers I did not wish to buy. My reflection caught me unaware in the pharmacy's window. Younger than I imagined myself to be, wide startled eyes watery from the cold. And then a realisation, warm like a mother's embrace, soft like the afternoon breeze in Ibn Zaydun's poem. I remembered why the Ostrich's bride had seemed familiar. She was a younger version of myself.

The Boy from the Kebab Shop

T he sign was on the door of the computer room.

Muslim Students' Society
FUND RAISING FOR KOSOVO
TALK & DINNER
Time: Tonight 6:00pm
Venue: Chaplaincy Centre

Dina went for the food. She arrived late and walked in as some people were leaving. Those who hadn't yet left were finishing their dinner, eating curry and rice off paper plates with plastic spoons. Not everyone was sitting around a table; some were sitting on chairs with plates on their laps, some were sitting on the floor. A few children ran around, climbed on the chairs and jumped off. The majority of people in the room were young students, though there were some mature students and a few middle-aged. Many of the girls were wearing headscarves, some were wearing shalwar-khamis, others like Dina wore the student outfit of jeans, sweat-shirt and outrageous shoes. She joined the queue for the dinner. It was not a long queue.

Kassim scooped the lumpy, unpopular rice from a crate (which

51

was actually a plastic box for storing toys), put it on a paper plate and said again, 'We've run out of chapattis.' With a soup ladle, he dished out curry from a huge pot. The last spoonfuls were thick with bits of chicken and pulverised potatoes. For the third time that evening, a student cut the queue and dumped his uneaten food in front of Kassim.

'I can't eat this rice.' The student wore an Adidas sweatshirt and glasses, 'It's not cooked. Look at it, stuck in lumps . . .'

'I'm sorry . . .' Kassim scooped the last piece of cucumber from the salad bowl and gave the plate to the young boy who was standing in front of Dina in the queue. The boy gave him a five-pound note and Kassim stuffed it in a Flora margarine container that was full of coins and notes. The boy didn't want any change.

'Give me chapattis instead of the rice,' said the student.

'We've run out of chapattis.'

'You've run out of chapattis, you're running out of chicken, what sort of organising is this. Every single function we have, there's something or other wrong with the food. You people can never get it right.' He walked away, hungry and angry.

Kassim put rice on Dina's plate. He stirred the ladle in the pot of curry searching for a piece of chicken. He said, 'It's mostly gravy now.'

'Doesn't matter.' She noticed that he looked scruffy and clean at the same time. Scruffy because of his beard and longish hair.

'I've found a wing,' he looked up at her. 'I'm sorry there's no salad left.'

She shrugged and put two pounds fifty into the Flora box.

Now that there was no one else to serve, Kassim wiped the table, put away the unused paper plates and the bag of plastic spoons. He shook open a black rubbish bag and started to move around the room, picking up empty paper plates and cups. Basheer was stacking up the chairs. Heavily built and with greying hair, it always surprised Kassim how quickly and efficiently he worked.

'Did the complaint reach you?' Kassim asked.

Basheer nodded and continued with his work.

'Well?'

'There has to be complaints. *Al-hamdullilah* the auction raised a thousand pounds. And they still haven't counted the donations yet. It's been a success.'

Basheer's wife, Samia, interrupted them. She carried a large plastic bowl. Her one-year-old son clung at her skirt, whining. 'We'll put all the leftovers here and then give it to the birds. We can't throw all this away.' She put the bowl on one of the tables.

True enough, the chicken bones were clean but most of the plates had remains of rice. Kassim began pushing the uneaten rice into the bowl before dumping the paper plate into the bag. As he moved away he heard Samia say to Basheer, 'Leave these chairs for Kassim; you'll just make your back worse.'

Kassim reached the table next to where Dina was sitting. 'Did you like the talk early on?' he asked her.

'I missed it.'

He nodded. 'Me too, I was cooking the rice.'

'It's good,' she said, swallowing another mouthful. She was not discerning. Her mother, Shushu, rarely cooked proper meals because she was always on a diet. Shushu imposed these diets on her daughter too who was even more overweight. The dieting made Dina continuously peckish, uneasy. She often binged on crisps and Mars bars, and the diets inevitably failed but they were never officially abandoned. Dieting had become a way of life, part of the house, part of the mother–daughter relationship. Whenever Dina found an opportunity like tonight, away from her mother, she devoured the food, indiscriminately.

'I work in a kebab shop,' Kassim said. He nodded towards Basheer, 'He owns the shop. The meal tonight is a donation.'

Kassim pushed more paper plates in the bag and tied it up. He hauled the bag away.

By the time Dina finished her plate, the only people left in the room were Kassim, Basheer, another man, Samia and her toddler. Most of the chairs were stacked and put away; Kassim was wiping the tables with a cloth and the other man had started to hoover. The machine was old and the hose kept breaking off.

Because they were the only two women in the room, Samia came over and sat with Dina. With her son whining and the sound of the vacuum cleaner, conversation was difficult. Samia picked up her baby and shifted her chair so that her back was to the men in the room.

'Tell me if anyone comes,' she said and Dina couldn't quite understand what she meant.

She did a minute later when Samia lifted up her jumper, pulled down her bra and started to breastfeed her baby. He became instantly quiet – this was what he had been whining for.

As an average British girl of seventeen, Dina had seen plenty of nudity but she had never seen a woman breastfeed a baby. Now she was taken aback, slightly repulsed. Samia was a large woman; her loose clothes gave her a tomboyish look. The white scarf that covered her hair made her eyes dark and luminous. She smelt faintly of sweat and cooking spices. Feeding her baby, she definitely did not look like an antiseptic mum in a television ad for Pampers. The baby, Dina thought, was too old for this. She could hear him breathing from the effort of sucking, could hear him swallow, draw in the flow of milk, swallow. She looked away, not wanting this intimacy, shrinking away from what was fleshy and vulnerable. In this modern age, Dina was not psyched up for birth or motherhood. C++ was on her mind and should she or should she not like her best friend Alanna pierce her tongue or tattoo a butterfly on her arm.

Samia suddenly became chatty and inquisitive. Questions that Dina answered dully because she was mesmerised by the child who was now dozing in his mother's arms, sucking himself to sleep, well fed.

This was the information that Samia got out of Dina. Dina was an IT student; her mother was Egyptian, her father Scottish. Her father had died recently from lung cancer. Her mother worked as a beautician in a department store. Dina's ties to Islam were fragile and distant. No, she had never been to Egypt. Shushu's family had disowned her when she married a Scot.

'Half Scottish, half Arab,' murmured Samia. 'That's like Kassim, but he's the other way round. His mother is Scottish and his father Moroccan.' Her baby let go of her nipple and suddenly snored loudly, his mouth wide open. Samia laughed and hitched up her bra, kissed her baby's forehead and pulled down her jumper. Dina laughed too, it made her feel less embarrassed.

Dina walked into the sitting room, which was dark except for the light of the television screen. Shushu was slumped on the sofa as if asleep. There was a bottle of gin on the coffee table, a glass, a packet of Panadol. Dina bent down over her mother, knelt down and touched her hair.

'Mum.'

Shushu's response was garbled. She turned her head away. There was mascara running down her face. Her breath, when she started to cry, was dry and sour.

'Mum what happened? Did anything happen at work?'

Shushu shook her head.

Dina sat on the floor and waited. She watched the black and white Egyptian film that was on Nile TV. It would have been romantic or at least sad if Shushu was mourning her husband. But she had despised him and despised him until he had shrivelled into his grave. The good-looking *khawagah*, who had pursued and enchanted her in the Gezira Club, whisked her off her feet and away from her family, had brought her to a drab life, in a drab place. In Scotland, he lost the charisma that Africa bestows on the white man, and became the average, kind-hearted father that Dina grew up with. A man who liked to go the pub, watch the football, dream of winning the lottery and not much else. Shushu expressed it now. She raised her arm up in the air, unsteadily, but brought it down hard to thud on the carpet.

'Whoosh.' It was all in that word, in the slender arm falling down onto the carpet. 'Everything shrunk when your father brought me here.'

'Go to bed,' said Dina. She had heard all this before; none of it was new. 'Don't get yourself all upset.'

'My sister won't send me the money.'

'That's why you're upset?'

'I spoke to her on the phone,' Shushu sat up on the couch. Her hair was dishevelled. 'My sister has a flat in Mohandisin. She has two maids doing all the work. Imagine two maids. And yet she grudges me, what is actually mine, my inheritance from my mother.'

'Hmm.'

'It was a black day when I first saw your father.'

They watched the film until the end. Nile TV was good for Dina because it had English subtitles on most of the films and so she could follow them. Sometimes, but not often, Shushu would make comments about the actors or the plot, give Dina snippets of information about Egyptian culture. Comments that were acerbic and surprisingly witty. Dina treasured them.

'Mum,' said Dina hesitantly, when the word *Al-nihaya* filled the screen accompanied by a flourish of music. 'I phoned AA. They said I could come with you to a meeting, if you were too shy to go on your own.'

Shushu waved her hand dismissively. She lay down again on the couch.

'Why not? It would be like Weight Watchers – once a week.'

'Leave me alone,' Shushu's voice was tired, withdrawn.

Kassim looked for Dina the next day at college and found her in the computer room. He sat on the swivel chair next to her and watched her as she worked. She was wearing glasses. He gave her the samosas he had made for her. Chicken and vegetable samosas in a greasy brown bag. Her gratitude and pleasure were the reward he wanted. She ate them straightaway even though there was a sign saying that no food or drink was allowed into the computer room.

'I'm thinking of getting married,' Kassim said to Basheer. Five o'clock was quiet in the kebab shop. Things picked up after six and got brisker. The busiest time was when the pubs closed at eleven.

'That's great,' said Basheer. His eyes lit up as they did whenever he was deeply pleased.

'Still at the early stages,' said Kassim.

'*Insha Allah* the wife you choose will be good and calm like you and a strong believer,' he put his arm around Kassim.

'Thanks Basheer.'

'What for?'

'I've learnt a lot from you.'

Basheer shrugged and continued to hook alternate meat and green peppers onto a skewer. Although Kassim regularly attended the Reverts class at the mosque and learnt a lot, it was the daily contact with Basheer that had made him live Islam. It was working with Basheer, day in day out, through the mundane and the significant that had made Islam a rhythmic reality, a feasible way of living. Kassim had not had a religious upbringing. His Moroccan father had given him a Muslim name, circumcised him at the age of eight months, and took him a total of five times to the children's mosque school. After that secular life had taken over. Kassim's Scottish mother had no interest in religion and no Muslim friends. She was close to her large Aberdeenshire family and Kassim grew up with Christmas and Hogmanay. Most times he felt he was just like his cousins, sometimes, though, he was conscious of his weird name and his father who spoke English with a funny accent. Kassim grew up a confident, happy child. Yet sometimes an incident would occur or someone would behave in a way that would make him stop, stand still and think, 'This canna be right.' He would not dwell on it too much, though. It was not in his nature to brood. Instead, he would shrug the feeling off and continue. It was Judo that awakened his dormant Muslim identity. Judo lessons that were held in the city, away from his suburban home. He took the bus into town and his mother and cousins thought the Judo was just a teenage whim that would pass. But he made friends with some of the other boys in the class. Arab boys who recognised his name straightaway.

Dina stood in front of the kebab shop and looked through the window. She could see Kassim cutting the doner kebab. He was wearing an apron. She watched him turn around to serve a customer, a tired-looking man with wispy hair combed over his balding forehead. Kassim sliced a loaf of pitta bread, put the doner kebab inside it. He held up a bottle of tahina. The man nodded. Kassim squeezed tahina into the sandwich. When the man shook his head at the offer of salad and hot sauce, Kassim put the sandwich into a brown paper bag. He wiped his hands on his apron, took a note from the man and opened the till. It was when he looked up as the man was leaving, that he saw Dina. She saw his smile, surprised and happy to see her. It gave her this wide, good feeling that she associated with him; subconscious images of the sky rippling open, a healthy organ deep under the skin, succulence. He opened the door for her and said, 'Salaamu Alleikum'.

It made her feel a bit self-conscious, this specific Muslim greeting, new words she was not used to. She did not reply, only smiled and said, 'I was just passing by.'

Minutes later she was sitting down at one of the two tables that were in the shop. Kassim got her a piece of doner pizza, a samosa and an onion bhaji. He refused to let her pay. Samia came in with her baby in a pushchair. She remembered Dina and kissed her hello. Samia and Basheer spoke in loud Arabic, which Dina couldn't understand. Kassim interrupted them, 'Basheer, can I get a break, half an hour or so? I'll make it up later. Promise.'

When she finished eating, they went out for a walk.

They walked along the beach. The sea was dark denim and sleek dolphins rose from the water and twisted back into it again. The wind blew Dina's hair and the smell of the sea raised her spirits. She became talkative and bright. When they sat down on the sand, she leaned and kissed Kassim on the cheek, ran her fingers through his hair and beard. She expected him to turn round and kiss her, but he blushed, and though he did not move away from her, she sensed him tense and so she was the one who moved away.

He mumbled something about marriage.

'Even to kiss?' Her voice was soft. A dog barked in the background and the cries of the seagulls were jarring and rude.

He didn't reply and she felt sorry for him in the way that people feel sorry for the crippled and the paralysed. It was a kind of pity that drew them apart rather than close.

'Someone's coming round to pick up clothes for Kosovo. I'm going to give him Dad's things.'

Shushu didn't reply and poured herself another drink. Ever since they had installed the satellite dish and Shushu could see the

Egyptian channel, she watched it all weekend. She enjoyed it thoroughly even though it sometimes made her envious and homesick.

When Kassim came, Shushu was sulky and refused to speak to him. She pressed the remote control and the room was drowned in the voice of the Egyptian singer Wardah. 'We can sit in the kitchen,' Dina said to Kassim.

They sat in the kitchen. Dina started to show him her father's clothes. She had washed them, ironed them and folded them up neatly. She had spent hours doing that with Shushu sneering in the background.

Kassim started to tell her about Kosovo, about the Muslim villages hit, about people losing their homes and living in camps. She started to cry and he thought she was moved by what he had been saying. But she had not really taken in what he was saying; it was all so far away. She cried for her father, she was for the first time freely grieving. Kassim and what he was saying about Kosovo took her away from her mother's bitterness, her mother's opinion of her father.

Gin made Shushu crave olives. Naughty olives that were full of calories. She resisted then left the television to get the jar from the fridge. She discovered Dina sobbing and Kassim looking embarrassed.

'Why are you crying?' She turned to Kassim, 'You made her cry. Why is she crying? What did you do to upset her?'

'Nothing, Mrs McIntyre.'

'Then why is she crying?'

'Mum, I'm okay,' said Dina breathing. 'It's nothing. He didn't make me cry.'

'Why is he here anyway?' Shushu whispered under her breath, but it was audible. She got the jar of green olives out of the fridge and sat with them at the table.

'I'd better be off,' said Kassim standing up.

'See you.' Dina felt glued to her chair, heavy and unattractive.

'Yeah, see you.'

'Goodbye Mrs McIntyre.'

Shushu didn't answer and instead twisted open the jar of olives. Kassim picked up the black bin liner that was full of clothes and saw himself out, quietly closing the kitchen door.

Shushu dipped her fingers into brine and popped an olive in her mouth. Dina followed, then wiped her eyes with the back of her hand. 'I forgot to give him Dad's suits.'

For all her faults, Shushu had a mother's instinct. She sensed the threat of Kassim. 'So that's the boy from the kebab shop . . .'

'I like him.' Dina bit into another olive. The green ones were always more bitter than the black.

'You'll end up in a horrible council flat with racist graffiti on the wall.' There was no menace in Shushu's voice, just disappointment.

They did not move until they had finished all the olives in the jar. Only the brine remained, wasted vinegar speckled green with bits of olive.

The bag of clothes was heavy and Kassim took the bus instead of walking. It did not take him long to get over the shock of Shushu. He had seen her type late at night in the kebab shop, women ravaged by dieting and trying too hard. He pitied them, as if they were ill or handicapped. It was the kind of pity that made them distant, far removed. If Kassim was given to irony he would have compared Dina's Muslim mother to his own Western mother and laughed. His mother was conservative and sedate, prim and houseproud. But Kassim was not given to irony or despair. He believed that wrong could be made right, nothing was impossible and things could improve.

By the time he reached the kebab shop and put the clothes at the back with all the other things that were going in the truck to

Kosova, he had forgotten all about Shushu. The rice he cooked that night was a success. There were congratulations from Basheer. 'You've done it, Kassim. Every grain of rice can't stand the touch of its brother.' They laughed and high fived.

The next day Dina took her father's suits to the kebab shop. She got a lift in a friend's car and chatted all the way proudly about Kassim, Kosovo and the clothes. The fact that her father's clothes were going to Kosovo gave his death a profoundness it hadn't had before. In the kebab shop Basheer was busy serving customers. It was the first time for Dina to say 'Salaamu Alleikum'. The self-consciousness passed when Basheer replied. He saw the clothes she was carrying and said, 'Thank you, this is a big help. Give them to Kassim, he's at the back.'

She had never walked before through the 'For Staff Only' door. The excitement of knowing she was going to see Kassim again, after a few steps, after a few minutes. And she was not an outsider today, not a customer, but one of 'them', pushing open a private door, as if she were Samia, as if she was part of the family too.

It was dark and she paused until her eyes adjusted. She was in a narrow corridor. Stacks of soft drinks came into view, a pile of chairs; in bulk aluminium foil containers, plastic plates, paper napkins, bin liners. There were also piles of the things that were going to Kosovo. Nappies, blankets, shoes, jumble, toys, tins of food and packets of pasta. She walked a few steps. Coats and jackets were hanging on a row of hooks that ran along the side of a wall. She found a free hook and hung up her father's suits. She heard a sneeze and said, 'Kassim?' But there was no reply. A small room, not much bigger than a wardrobe, opened out after the row of jackets. She heard a faint whisper and the rustle of movement and knew he was there.

'Kassim?'

It was then that her heart started beating, her blood turned cold, because he was not within arm's reach, because he was down on the ground, and it was a shock to see him like that, so still and grovelling, not searching for something that had fallen, not answering her. It was fear that she felt. And wanting him to reassure her, and wanting the shock to go away. Why was he like that, his forehead, nose and hands pressed onto the floor, why . . .? He sat up and did not speak to her, did not acknowledge her presence. Descended though Dina was from generations of Muslims, she had never seen anyone praying. On television, yes, or a photo in a schoolbook, but not within arm's reach, not in the same room, not someone she knew, someone that she loved. When she understood, her pulse rate dulled back to normal, her fear turned to embarrassment. 'I'm sorry,' she mumbled and turned away. If she had accidentally pushed the toilet door open and found him sitting on the loo, she would have apologised in the same way. Like seeing Samia that day feeding her baby, the intimacy of it, something fleshy and vulnerable.

Dina stumbled out of the dim corridor to the bright light of the shop, customers milling round, barbecue smoke and the happy ring of the till. She walked out to the street, to the cold normality of traffic, high heels hitting the tarmac, cars parked on the road. She stood very still, her back to the kebab shop, her eyes glued to the tyre of a parked car and seeing nothing. He was inviting her to his faith, her faith really, because she had been born into it. He was passing it on silently by osmosis and how painful and slow her awakening would be! If she now waited long enough, he would come out looking for her. If she went home, he would know that she was not keen on his lifestyle, did not want to change her own.

She paused on the pavement, hesitating between the succulent mystic life he promised, and the peckish unfulfilment of her parent's home.

Tuesday Lunch

N adia is eight and she can read now. She can read the lunch menu for today, Tuesday, stuck on the door of the gym. The gym is used as a dining room during lunch. Tables with benches fastened to them cover the white lines on the floor where the children bounce balls and slide bean bags. Now as the children chatter and crowd in the queue, as the delicious smells waft through from the kitchen amidst the clutter of spoons and trays, Nadia finds it hard to believe that this is the gym room. If she were to take her skirt off right now, stand in her white shorts, run or jump, how wrong that would be, how out of place. Yet in the afternoon this is what she will be doing and there will be no smells of food, no plates, no tables and if you start to eat something right in the middle of gym, how naughty you would be. These thoughts give her a feeling of pride; she is older now, she understands the difference, she can behave in a correct way and as a blessing, as a reward, blend with everyone else, not stand apart. For this was bad behaviour, this was naughtiness, being pointed out, the centre of attention, the general disapproval for being different. You play quietly, you are alone in your own world with imaginary friends. And then if you do something wrong, even if you don't mean to, the peace is shattered. Her mother snaps in irritation, the child's voice rises, 'Mrs Benson, Nadia broke my pencil.'

Yet knowing that she can leave the queue, that she can let go of her tray and run pretending it was time for gym, that nothing was physically restraining her, filled her with a thrill. A fear that somehow the control will slip, that she will slide to a younger, innocent age, only that now forgiveness will not come so easily as it did years before. 'You knew you were doing something wrong,' Lateefa would say pinching her arm 'It's not that you didn't know, you knew, so *why* did you do it?' Nadia is now eight and she knows that wilful disobedience is not something that adults forgive easily.

The menu is written in black in Mrs Hickson's handwriting. She hangs it up on Monday and it shows the lunches for the whole week. Sometimes before Nadia goes to sleep at night, she lies awake and tries to remember the menu for the rest of the week, listing the items one by one. Monday night is the most challenging, Thursday night the easiest. Today, Tuesday, is Chicken Risotto, Pork Pie, Mashed Turnips, Boiled Potatoes, Tomato and Nut Salad, Black Forest Gâteau, and Fruit Yoghurt. Nadia knows it must be the Chicken Risotto for her and then she has a choice of the vegetables and dessert.

Nadia likes chicken. At home Lateefa buys halal chicken, travelling by bus every week to the Pakistani butcher in Finchley Road, and carrying four of them home in one of the green Marks & Spencer bags that she collects. Chicken Risotto, the potatoes (not the turnips, definitely not the turnips) and the cake, this is what she will take. And Mrs Hickson knows about the pork, so when it is Nadia's turn, Mrs Hickson will give her the chicken with what Nadia calls her giant fork. Mrs Hickson knows about the pork because Lateefa had told her. Lateefa had told everyone: the headmaster, who was very polite; Mrs Benson, Nadia's teacher, who said that Nadia can very well read the menu and there is always a choice (a reply Lateefa found unconvincing); and finally Mrs Hickson herself, who showed great interest and concern.

However, Lateefa argued later to Hamdy, if I saw one of these poor children whose crazy parents are vegetarians eating meat, I wouldn't stop him, would I? 'You would if it was your job to do so,' he said and promptly fell asleep. But just to make sure, she decided to bribe them, the headmaster, the teacher and especially Mrs Hickson. They of course never imagined they were being bribed. The headmaster got an Egyptian alabaster ashtray and an ivory letter opener. His teenage daughter, horrified at the thought that an African elephant was slain for its tusks, threw it in the attic, where it languished among jigsaw puzzles with missing pieces and headless dolls. The ashtray accidentally found its way to the school jumble sale (none of the family smoked), where Lateefa winced when she saw it and paid thirty pence to take it back home.

Mrs Benson was happier with her present, a pair of earrings with a pharaonic design, while Mrs Hickson was thrilled with her cotton cushion covers. She bought a filling for them and scattered them on her double bed. She thought they gave the room a somewhat mysterious, 'ethnic' look. 'I would love to go to Cairo one day,' she told Lateefa, 'my father was there during the war.' Lateefa told her the joke about the Egyptian village where suddenly all the babies born had blond hair and blue eyes. There was apparently a British garrison stationed nearby during the war. But Mrs Hickson did not laugh.

It is not Mrs Hickson serving out the hot meal this Tuesday and Nadia suddenly finds herself facing a young woman she has never seen before, a woman who is asking 'Pork pie or chicken?' And to Nadia it is as if the whole room has changed or that she, Nadia, has changed. If she answers 'pork pie' or even just the 'pie', no need to say the forbidden word, just say 'pie', this new dinner lady will not be surprised, she will pick one up with the giant tweezers and put it on Nadia's plate. It will sit with the potatoes and the salad. But where is Mrs Hickson? She might suddenly appear. 'No pork for Nadia,' she will say, looking behind her shoulders and the new dinner lady will turn with a sigh, a slight irritation. 'Well why didn't you say so, child?' and give Nadia the chicken.

Then Nadia asks about Mrs Hickson. The children behind her are impatient, the lady's hand is poised in the air holding the tweezers. But Nadia must ask, she swallows and speaks. 'Off ill,' the reply. Mrs Hickson has never been ill, not before, and Nadia feels there must be a pause, a time to ponder, a time to take in the newness.

Mrs Hickson is at home nursing a bladder infection, clutching a hot-water bottle to her stomach, drinking water to flush the germs out of her system. She glances at the clock, 12 noon, and does not think of Nadia, or that she would be now standing dishing out the meals. She only thinks, *Dammit, three more hours until I take the second tablet; when will these antibiotics start to work?*

'If you don't want a hot meal, you can have cheese and biscuits with the potatoes,' the lady says, already looking at the boy behind Nadia in the queue.

'Pie,' whispers Nadia. 'I'll have the pie.'

It tastes like chicken. It doesn't taste bitter or sour. Not like the other things Lateefa forbids her to taste like perfume and orange peel. It tastes like ordinary food. Nadia pushes ketchup on it with her knife and it tastes better with the ketchup. The other children talk while they are eating, a normal day, a normal lunch hour. Yesterday Nadia was like them, but today the lunch break seems infinite, real, glittering. Tracy, Nadia's best friend, is eating the Chicken Risotto. Tracy, who on other days ate pork pies while Nadia watched and wondered. Tracy, who brings bacon-flavoured crisps to school and Nadia doesn't try them. Today, of all days, Tracy is eating the Chicken Rissoto. And Nadia feels a sudden dislike for her friend.

*   *   *

In the classroom, after lunch, it is time for mathematics. Tracy is not good at maths, not like Nadia and while Nadia divides, Tracy is still multiplying. Nadia's workbook is neat, she works quickly moving her lips as if she is talking to herself. When she finishes a page Mrs Benson checks it and stamps a picture of a boy rushing past on a skateboard. 'Keep it up,' the slogan above his head says. Sixteen divided by four, twelve divided by three, fifteen divided by five. Easy. And Nadia worries a little about what she would do if the sixteen were divided by five, if the picture in the workbook showed three children with ten sweets to share among them. It wouldn't work then; they wouldn't be able to share. Nadia pushes a feeling away, a tired feeling it is such a long time since lunch, since breakfast. But she can't think about that and can't even think of the chocolate bar she and Lateefa will share when she gets home from school.

There is a bad feeling in her chest and in her throat and she wants it to go away. Ten divided by two, six divided by three, eighteen divided by six. She is stuck; eighteen divided by six . . . if it was divided by nine that would have been easy but six, eighteen divided by six. Maybe it is one of those numbers that couldn't be divided, like the three children couldn't share ten sweets. The numbers seem jumbled now on the page; time seems so slow. Nadia thinks she should get up, walk up to Mrs Benson bending over Tracy's red hair. When she looks my way I will speak to her, thinks Nadia, and she puts her head on the workbook. It feels cool to her forehead. Her forehead is damp. The black numbers on the page loom close to her. The boy on the skateboard grins maliciously and she closes her hurting eyes.

'Nadia, Nadia,' Mrs Benson's voice filters through and Nadia lifts her face up, swallows but it is too late. A gush, the sound of a tap opening, a flood on the workbook, on Nadia's lap, on Mark's pencils, a speck of potato on Brian's left arm. And on the soaked boy with the skateboard, a pink remnant of pork pie, his face still grinning through, 'Keep it up.' And Nadia keeps it up when Mrs Benson with remarkable agility positions the waste-paper basket strategically in front of her. Impossible to stop, even when Brian says 'Ukk, Ukk, Ukk', and continues to say it, even with Tracy spluttering with laughter, covering her mouth with her hands, her knees clenched together, and even while Mark whines gently, 'Mrs Benson I need a new pencil.'

There is no relief. Intervals but no relief. In one of those intervals Nadia is led to the toilet. Mrs Benson is kind, helping her clean her jumper, telling her to wash her face, not angry, not shouting. Nadia is afraid she will be angry; the mess in the class – who was going to clean it? and the workbook – what will happen to the workbook?

In the toilet the rest of her lunch floods out, easier now, not so thick and clogged, smoother. The red of ketchup, orange juice, lots of orange juice. And at home, when Lateefa finally picks her up and they go home, there is nothing left. She retches, her stomach squeezes itself, but there is nothing left, just a dull, still pain in her muscles. A drained feeling, her body trembling.

'Get into bed, Nadia, sleep and you'll feel better; I won't let you eat anything else today. Tomorrow Insha Allah you'll be better.' In her pyjamas Nadia feels clean; her room smells nice; the sheets are cool and comforting.

'What is it that you ate that made you so sick? What did you have for lunch?'

'Chicken,' says Nadia, her nose in the pillow, her eyes closed, and then after a while 'Mrs Hickson was off ill today.'

'What else did you eat?'

'Black Forest Gâteau.'

'What's that?'

'A cake Mama, a chocolate cake.'

'It must have been the cream then. Old cream, bad for your

stomach. Go to sleep now; I'm going downstairs.' Relief, an empty stomach, at last relief and sleep will come easy now.

Nadia opens the cloakroom cupboard but it is not a cloakroom any more. It is her aunt Salwa's flat in Cairo. It doesn't look exactly like Tante Salwa's flat. It is more untidy, darker, narrow like the cloakroom. Her cousin Khalid is sitting on a chair, looking out of the window. Nadia climbs into his lap and he puts his arms around her, and his cheek rubs against her chin. She asks him what he is looking at without speaking, and he shows her the busy street below, the man blowing his horn selling candy floss, another with a large rack balanced in front of his bicycle filled with pitta bread. And Mrs Hickson standing alone in front of a table covered with pork pies, a table like the ones that Nadia eats lunch on at school. The giant tweezers in her hands, a placard with the picture of the boy on the skateboard showing the price, eighteen divided by six pence. Three, says Nadia to Khalid, three pence, but it is as if Khalid can't hear her. No one is going to buy these pies, he says.

Nadia is awake and hungry. The house is silent and dark. She has missed Children's BBC, missed Hamdy's key turning the lock on the front door. She has missed dinner. Lateefa will have told Hamdy about her being ill and sudden tears come to Nadia's eyes imagining how anxious and sad he must have been. He will have opened the door and looked at her while she slept, the way parents do on TV.

Tomorrow at school they will call her Nauseous Nadia, they will write Nozeus Nadia, NN for short. She will be hurt and ashamed. She will hope that they will forget the whole thing like magic, as if it didn't take place. But now she is hungry.

She wanders to her parents' bedroom. She can hear Hamdy snoring. Lateefa wakes up as if she was not asleep, clear and lucid and bright as if she was waiting for Nadia. She holds her daughter's cheek against her own to check her temperature. Nadia puts her arms around her and Lateefa says she will make toast and that Nadia should go back to bed.

Nadia can smell the toast, the smell made more delicious by the stillness of the night, the hunger she feels. Lateefa brings the toast with jam and they both sit up on Nadia's bed, covering themselves with the pink and orange quilt. The toast has strawberry jam on it and it is sweet and warm. Lateefa feels soft and Nadia leans against her arms; she can smell the jam and the bread. She wonders why her mother looks so beautiful now in her sleeveless cotton nightdress, not like when she picks Nadia up from school.

They giggle, it doesn't matter about the crumbs falling on the bed. They drink tea without any milk. No milk for a bad stomach, Lateefa says. The mug of tea is too hot for Nadia to hold and Lateefa must hold it for her in between sips. Lateefa has been teaching her a short chapter from the Qur'an, *Surat El-Ekhlas*, for some days now and Nadia can say it all by herself. '*In the Name of Allah, the Compassionate, the Merciful. Say: He is Allah, the One and Only. Allah, the Eternal, the Absolute. He begetteth not, nor is He begotten and there is none comparable unto Him.*'

Lateefa kisses Nadia. 'Clever girl, not one mistake. When we go to Cairo you can show Khalid and Tante Salwa and they will be so proud of you.'

Now Lateefa takes the empty mugs away and it is time for Nadia to sleep. As sleep approaches, Nadia thinks that her mother must have cast a spell on all the wrong things Nadia should not do. Bewitched pork pies, so that even when she wanted them, they, on their own accord, rejected her.

Make Your Own Way Home

Friday Afternoon

I t is strange to visit Tracy in a nursing home. Somehow Nadia associates the words with the old and the infirm and Tracy has not yet said goodbye to her teens. But that is what the elegant gold letters say and when Nadia rings the bell she asks herself, But what else do you expect them to write on the front door?

Cosy, unobtrusive, the house is like any other in this quiet north London street. A quaint gate, a small front garden, and when she goes inside Nadia can see the back garden with a clothes line, a green lawnmower propped against the wooden fence of next door.

There are four women in the room. Tracy, three others and two empty beds. It's not one of our busy days, the nurse later says. The curtains separating the beds are open and Oprah Winfrey beams down from the TV which protrudes from the wall high above. Bullying is the topic of the show. Childhood victims of bullying are telling their stories to a sympathetic audience.

Tracy in a pink nightgown, lank hair, a little pale. No, it doesn't hurt much now; it did at first. We all had it done one after the other. I was first, then they brought me back here in a wheelchair.

She tells Nadia about the other women in the room. The oldishlooking woman is Irish, Mandy or Maggie; Tracy isn't sure. Her husband is sitting with her on the bed, they are laughing at the television show. The skinny woman with the permed hair, Kay. And the blonde with the great tan, she's come all the way from South Africa. She was far ahead of us, Tracy whispers; you can still see now how big her stomach is. And believe me, Nadia, she soaked her bed with blood.

The South African girl has a visitor, a similar-looking friend who arrives with flowers. Kay's boyfriend appears shortly after Nadia. Fat and reluctant he edges his way into the room, empty-handed. I should have brought flowers, thinks Nadia. But then she consoles herself with the thought that if she hadn't come, Tracy would have been the only one without a visitor.

Do you have change for the phone?

Tracy takes twenty pence and gets up slowly from the bed, shuffling her feet around in search for her slippers. When she walks to the door she holds her lower stomach with one hand and Nadia sees dark stains on her friend's nightgown.

Nadia lied to her parents to be here. Of course. What could she have told them? Long ago Lateefa unwittingly bestowed glamour on Tracy, making her friendship even more desirable. Lateefa said, That girl Tracy is no good. Don't be her friend any more. Perhaps she saw warning signs in the streak of colour on Tracy's lips, the awareness in her eyes. When Tracy wore a short skirt, she no longer crossed her bare legs carelessly like a child but did it deliberately with all the calm knowledge of an adult. She'll have a bad end, Lateefa said and Nadia knew that her mother's mind held images of the fallen women of the Egyptian cinema screen. The wrathful uncle from the south of Egypt stalking his niece with a loaded gun. Only blood could wash his family's dishonour. And off the screen, in urban Cairo where there were no guns, there would be shame. Lateefa could imagine the shame. Mothers get divorced for this kind of thing. Sisters remain unwed. Grandmothers go to their graves before their time, crushed by sorrow. A girl's honour is like a matchstick, break it and it can never be fixed.

Tracy has no gun-wielding uncle from the south. Her father will not divorce her mother because he already did so years ago. He went to Australia and Tracy's dream is that she will visit him there one day. She watches *Neighbours* with obsessive love, she has three stuffed koala bears in her bedroom.

Tracy threw a tantrum when the perfect blue circle showed up on the stick she dipped in her morning urine. She could not believe it; such a thing could not happen to her. And today is a kind of relief; it is over at last. Time to get back to normal, to start pretending that nothing has happened.

Her mother paid up the two hundred and fifty pounds without a fuss. Then she packed and drove with Tracy's stepfather and the twins to a house-swap holiday with a family in the Black Forest. The travel plans were made ages ago, house-swapping takes a long time to arrange and there was absolutely No Way they could cancel. And as Stepdad said, was it fair that the family's holiday be disrupted because of Tracy's carelessness?

So yesterday Tracy was counselled as the law prescribed, today she is to spend the night at the nursing home and next day she will go back to her everyday life. End of story.

They called me white trash. Oprah's guest says this and bursts into tears. Compassion gurgles around the studio audience. Only Oprah reigns plump and polished. The softest baby cheeks, coiffured, coated with a yellow designer suit.

Now the show reaches new heights: former bullies appear to confront those people whose childhood they ruined. Boos and hisses from the audience. Irish laughter from the bed in the corner. Nadia can see that Maggie and her husband are holding hands. I never get to see this show, she is saying to him. It's the time when the children are always watching their programmes on the other channel. But Nadia cannot laugh like them, her own childhood is still too close to her. She is moved by the pain unfolding before her on the screen. Was she bullied, did she ever bully anyone? Uneasy thoughts. And why is it that so many years later it is so easy to distinguish the bullies from their prey? Adult bodies surrounding the children of long ago. The years have changed nothing.

He wasn't there. Tracy gives the coins back to Nadia. Let's go upstairs. We're not allowed to smoke in here.

Upstairs is a bright room overlooking the front of the house. Oriel windows with seats all around, a high ceiling, sandwiches on a tray. Coffee, tea, a kettle. Magazines and pamphlets on the low coffee table, posters on the walls. 'Have You Considered Sterilisation?' . . . 'The Morning After Pill – Ask your GP about it'.

Nadia chews a cheese sandwich, makes tea, leafs through the pamphlets. So what are you going to use now Tracy, progesterone injections, the low-dose mini-pill, the IUD? She reads them out as if she is choosing lunch from a menu.

Shut up, Nadia.

Tracy lights her second cigarette, and for an instant the flame gives her features a delicate glow as if she is painted, not real. She snaps the match in her hand into two before she throws it in the ashtray.

They sucked it out. The vacuum roared and sucked and gobbled. It's a very loud noise, I told the nurse. Not really, she said, you must be imagining it. All the painkillers that you took. She held my hand and chatted to me to distract me. I lay down and it was like an initiation rite in those weird ceremonies they have in horror films. *The contents of your womb*, she called it. This is what they call it here. So many words for such a tiny thing.

Soon the others come upstairs one by one. More cigarettes, tea, coffee. These sandwiches are good . . . I'm so hungry the dinner I got was terrible. It was a mistake asking for the fish . . . They said we'll get breakfast in bed tomorrow . . . We'll be lucky if it is Rice Krispies, probably one piece of toast with jam . . .

In their nightdresses and with the unexpected sandwiches, there is almost a festive atmosphere in the room.

I had a scare two months ago, says Kay, my period came late, five days. It's strange that is. Last year exactly the same thing happened to a couple we know. My boyfriend was all stiff and disapproving. Said it was the wrong thing to do but now when he's in the same situation, it's all right. We came here last night so that he could pay because he couldn't come with me this morning. I nearly changed my mind then, I hated the look of this place.

I have four kids, Maggie says, I have asthma and look at my legs mottled with varicose veins. I couldn't face a fifth, had to come specially from Ireland for this.

And the golden beauty came all the way from Cape Town. The laws in South Africa are so backward, she says. I'll stay in London for a few more days; I've been here before but there are still things I'd like to see.

I've been dancing, jogging and I didn't miss my aerobics class. We even went hill-walking on the weekend, Kay smiles for the first time. I thought something would happen but I was fine; nothing ever happened. My boyfriend kept saying, come on walk faster, save us some money.

Everyone laughs.

Nadia imagines Fat Boyfriend puffing up the hill. *Two hundred and fifty pounds could take us to Majorca.*

My mum said the same thing, she tried everything to get rid of me, Tracy says, and it was so difficult in those days. She is laughing now, enjoying the conversation, the smoke-filled room, the feeling that her body no longer hurts like before.

I walked up the underground steps instead of taking the

escalator, adds the golden beauty, though it is not true; but she is eager to join in.

Now they boast of their fertility, brag of the way the lumped clot clung firmly inside them. The primitive urge to celebrate the ability to conceive. Only Maggie does not brag.

Some of my friends were so mean about this, says Kay. Why don't you get yourself sterilised one of them said. Imagine, what a thing to say.

Though she does not yet admit it to herself, Kay wanted him to propose marriage, commitment. Wanted him last night when they crept stealthily to the nursing home to turn back and say, No, forget it. But the fat man would not be prodded by the unscheduled, would not surrender, give way.

I'm taking a week off work, Kay goes on, hate the job anyway. Stupid boring job being a data operator. Is it by half past nine that we have to leave here tomorrow morning? He's coming to pick me up at nine.

Kay is talking more than the others. Pulling at her cigarette in tension, her thin legs crossed tightly together.

Chris told me, Make your own way home, Tracy, and Tracy laughs a little unevenly, shakes her red hair. Chris is my boyfriend, she adds to explain though there is no need. And he wasn't there when you phoned him, Nadia thinks.

Chris and Tracy. There was a Michael before Chris, an Ian before Michael. There was a time long ago when Tracy and Nadia were two little girls with the same Barbie dolls. They watched *Blue Peter* together. When they spoke, their words were spontaneous and pure ('Your tummy is brown . . . Why do you have red dots on your nose?'). In school they pushed each other into fits of giggles, finding humour in things they would not have found funny if they were alone. A girl's stocking, the janitor's moustache, a deviant white hair that grew right in the centre of Mrs Hickson's cheek and quivered when she spoke. An exchange of looks and

Tracy would start spluttering, covering her mouth with her hand, knees clenched together. Nadia's suppressed laughter would turn to shrill squeaks, a knot of pain in her chest. Then, and it did not happen overnight, but gradually, Tracy crossed to another world, entered a dimension that was neither adult nor child. Tracy's code became that of the magazines, the parameters of her new world boyfriends, dates, parties and first kisses.

Your parents are awful, Nadia. You're not allowed to do this, to do that. They are so inflexible. I mean this is London; people are free here, not some village on the Nile.

Cairo is a city, a big modern city. My father and mother never lived in a village.

Tracy is a broad-minded young girl. She knows people have different cultures, which means they dress differently, eat spicy food. No one told her there are different lenses through which you could look at the world. She is a tolerant girl, which means that at the whole Nadia issue she rolls her eyes skywards and sighs.

Don't you like anyone, Nadia? How about Ryan? He likes you. When he went cycling in Wales he sent you a letter.

No, he doesn't talk; he's too quiet. His handwriting is horrible.

Nadeem then, he's Muslim, your mummy would approve.

I don't like the way he keeps tossing his hair away from his eyes.

In Nadia's life there are crumpled notes which she picked up from a waste-paper basket. A smile of recognition, more than a year ago, across the aisle of an aeroplane. Plenty of dreams. All this she keeps from Tracy lest the spell be broken if she utters any words. Her dreams turn to drivel before Tracy's patronising eyes.

Perhaps she has come here today to gloat. To witness Tracy's punishment. Sit prim and virginal, pocket back the change for the failed telephone call.

She feels guilty at such thoughts, quashes them down. Reminds herself of friendship, digs deep for sympathy towards Tracy. Yet she is aware of the superfluity of her presence. She is out of place in this room, the only one not in a nightgown, the only one without an experience to swop. Why is she here then, flaunting the end of visiting hours? Why hasn't she gone home already? She is, in a strange way, enjoying herself.

The nurse comes in with sleeping pills. Swollen runny nose, a muffled voice. Sorry, ladies, I've got a bad cold.

Only Maggie has room for a sympathetic response. Tracy is eager for the pills. She isn't bothered to try the telephone again.

It is time for Nadia to go home.

A few stops on the underground, no need to change lines but she is still home a little late. I was at the library, she lies to her parents and feels again that odd disappointment when they believe without question what she says. And that evening she does not eat very much of the dinner Lateefa cooked. She is too full of cheese sandwiches.

Saturday Morning

Fat Boyfriend is in his car blocking the road when Nadia arrives. Fiddling with his CD player. Big car, a Granada. Fat Boyfriend has a good job in the city, a nice flat. Kay keeps it nice for him, scrubs the toilet bowl with disinfectant, presses his shirts better than they do at Sketchley.

She comes out now, a flamingo doing a quickstep. Pink leggings, pink stilettos. A wide belt around her waist, nipples angry against the tight tunic she is wearing. She blinks at Nadia through mascaraed lashes; yesterday's intimacy is forgotten.

Inside the home a new mood prevails. The nurse strips the sheets, eyes watery, hankies bulging in her pockets. I still have that terrible cold.

Golden beauty is squashed in her blue jeans, the flowers next to her bed limp and redundant. Tracy bustles about, blow-drying her hair, searching for her contact lenses. Cheerful now, energetic, ready to go home. Home to Chris, she has keys to his place. Her room at home with the koala bears is taken over by the house-swappers from the Black Forest.

Maggie's husband arrived early, shared her toast and jam. He is ready to carry her bag for her. Are you sure you got everything? Your toothbrush, your slippers? They are no longer in love, these two. They are peacefully addicted to each other. In equilibrium. And he did not sleep well in his bed and breakfast room the night before. Pity for her enveloped him; he lay conscious of the clammy sheets, the unfamiliar scents. Could not remember the last time he slept alone.

Maggie has time to greet Nadia, say goodbye to the nurse. Has space to think it's a treat not to have to make the beds, get the children's breakfast. Nice to get away. It's almost like a holiday really.

Now they leave to catch the ferry home. Pack some surprises for the children: a pencil with a rubber troll's head, two tiny London taxis, a Beefeater doll. They know what they left behind in the nursing home.

And Maggie is the epitome of why women are judged irrational. Through asthma attacks which squeeze her lungs, send her flinging windows wide open to gasp the icy night air, she remembers. She thinks, what if? In the midst of the strain of her children, the resentment that drains her at their unreasonable requests, she secretly grieves. Mourns the sweet smell of an orange-stained nappy, that prickle in her breasts when the milk gathers speed and sprays out, a whole personality she will never know.

Outside, the spring air is fresh for Nadia and Tracy. Tracy feels she has been indoors for too long. The sun is a little too bright, the noise of the traffic harsh. They walk to the tube station together.

Let me carry your bag.

No, I'm all right.

It seems to Tracy that the station is too far away. Was is that far when she came yesterday? Was it only yesterday that she walked in the opposite direction? It seems like a long time and she is now aware of a dull dragging pain inside her. She will need to rest when she gets home. Two weeks, that's what they said, until she will feel that she is back to normal.

Outside the station, she lights a cigarette, drops her bag on the floor. Leans against the stained wall.

Go ahead, don't wait for me.

It's okay. I'm not in a hurry.

Tracy is not the only one smoking outside the station. Others stand like her observing the ritual, preparing themselves for the descent under the ground.

So what are you going to do the rest of the day?

We might go to Islington.

Tracy smiles at the 'we' in Nadia's words. Nadia goes out with her parents more than any girl that Tracy knows. There is something childlike about Nadia, something pampered, though she could not be described as spoilt. She has a looked-after air about her.

Why Islington?

My mother wants to visit a lady whose husband is a student. The university hostels and flats are all there.

In the busy station, they walk down the few steps and buy their tickets. Back and forth people move; the Saturday-morning shoppers, elderly ladies with trolleys, women with pushchairs, young men with the earplugs of Walkmen around their throats. The ticket barriers suck the tickets, plastic doors swing open, the tickets are spat out. Open and shut go the doors, the escalators rattle and groan, their steps bristle and sweep down like the back of a Stegosaurus.

On the escalator, Nadia thinks that once you put your first foot
to go down, you cannot change your mind. It is difficult to walk up
again; there is someone standing on every step, there would be
people running down towards you. Even if it was empty, you
would look silly trying anyway. She used to do that when she was
young, play on the escalators in department stores, deliberately
struggle against their flow. Run quickly down the Up escalator,
pant up the Down until someone told her off and brought the
game to an end. Now she looks at the emergency Stop box, its red
wrinkled paper uninviting to touch. Pressing the box would bring
this giant, rattling machine to a standstill. It would be a dramatic
moment; people would perhaps fall from the jolt, hurt themselves.

She has never seen this happen. Now as she and Tracy stand in a
single file to the right while others walk quickly past them, she can
understand the reluctance that prevents the red box from being
pressed. There is a fear of stopping a process that has already been
set in motion.

They are half way down when a rushing man steps on Tracy's
foot. His briefcase brushes against her knees. She begins to cry and
the escalator keeps on descending, down everyone goes, under the
ground. For Tracy the ads on the side wall merge together in a blur
of tears. Musicals, the latest Michael Jackson album, Big Mac. Only
when they reach the bottom does Nadia notice.

What's wrong?

Nothing.

Why are you crying?

I don't know.

People walk past them. The sound of footsteps is like an endless
march, the indefatigable continuity of life. Nadia and Tracy are the
only ones standing at the bottom, where no one needs to stand.
There is not even a busker today filling the station with songs.
People are making a choice now: left northward, right southwards.

Nadia and Tracy should go right, follow the woman with the

beads in her hair south, follow the man with the tweed jacket holding his son's hand, the old woman with mauve hair. Instead they stand and Tracy rummages automatically in her bag, remembers the smoking ban and gives up. Leans on the wall, wipes her tears with the back of her hand.

Nadia is conscious of all the sounds around her, all the bustle of the station. Tracy is crying and Nadia is thinking we must have missed a train by now.

Are you in pain? Should we go back?

No just cramps, like period pains. They told me I would get them.

Pity for Tracy is superseded by illumination. Nadia can see the silver drop earring nestle in Tracy's earlobe, entwined by a single stray hair. She can see Tracy's eyebrow ruffled, the little hairs disturbed, askew. Nadia can see Tracy's womb. Bewildered, its mouth agape in a round full O. It murmurs and drones reproach. Pulses its defeat, retreats. Grudgingly contracts, adjusts. Sheds, expels, but there is little left to shed.

Try and feel pity for Tracy. Perhaps her tears are the tears of remorse, the tears of regret. Perhaps she lingers here under the ground so as not to go back to him. Back to the Chris who said, Make your own way home, Tracy.

Chris is younger than Tracy. Just a little younger. He delivers pizzas on a motorcycle. Tracy thinks he looks good in his motorcycle gear, better than he does without it. Looks better with the helmet and all the leather blackness. Chris sometimes forgets his gloves with the delivered pizzas and has to go back to ring the doorbells of customers. Mumbles for them back, bounces his weight from foot to foot. His eyes shift beneath a long fringe. He does not mean to be unkind when he tells Tracy to make her own way home. He has known her for five months.

You can come home and stay with us, says Nadia, until your

parents come back. Or maybe my dad could get you a cheap ticket to join them in Germany.

No, says Tracy, no. She is surprised by Nadia's offer. She can't understand why Nadia said that. Come on, let's go.

To continue is easier than to repent. Tracy is like the imprisoned thief whose only regret is that he was caught. When the doors of the train slide open, she will ride to Chris's flat, but be careful, really careful that she is not caught again, caught and taken to the nursing home.

Why doubt what the magazines encourage? She was just unlucky that's all. Here, right in front of them as the train pulls away, there is a poster of two handsome people, happy in the sunshine. The girl is blonde with a tan; she wears a green bathing suit. 'Be Safe this Summer with Durex' is the command. That ad with its clean sea and sand must be the truth then, not the vacuum that roared and sucked and gobbled.

Nadia thinks of how her mother can be both right and wrong at the same time. In Tracy's family there were no guns and maybe even no shame. Lateefa's Egyptian fears have no place in London. Here, the furious uncle was substituted by a stepfather who went away on holiday, who could eat Wurst and drink beer and sleep soundly at night while Tracy bore her own pain. And shame was substituted by the sense of inconvenience, washed by a facile night at the nursing home.

She used to envy Tracy, envy her and listen to her talk of Chris or Michael or Ian. She used to feel childish next to Tracy, lesser, small. Is she still ready to envy her now after she has seen behind the worldliness? There might have been no guns at the nursing home, but there was still blood.

When friendships run their course there are no rituals of mourning. There are no tears. There is not even a premonition of finality. So in the train as Tracy and Nadia sit in front of a woman in a sari reading the last pages of a library book, a man with a mermaid tattooed on his arm, they promise each other meetings and telephone calls. They will meet in college after the Easter break. Tracy wants to get a job with the Body Shop during the holidays, she will tell Nadia what it is like. Nadia will work in her father's travel agency; she will get Tracy brochures of Australia. They are not insincere in their promises but they will not keep them.

After three stops Nadia says goodbye, leaves Tracy to continue further south, change trains and head east. Alone Nadia can walk fast, run up the escalators. *Make your own way home, Tracy.*

In the small garden near the station, Nadia sits and watches a tramp rummage and mutter over the contents of the rubbish bin. She does not really want to look at the pigeons, but she does, not wanting the tramp to think she is staring at him. The pigeons are sick in this garden; they are bloated and lazy. They waddle about gorging themselves on the remnants of crisps and cigarette butts and all the things they were not created to eat. Near Nadia's foot a pigeon pecks at the dark bubbly liquid oozing out of a Diet Coke can. She stamps her foot to frighten it away, but the bird is placid, shrugs its wings, cooes and continues to drink.

The Museum

A t first Shadia was afraid to ask him for his notes. The earring
made her afraid. And the straight long hair that he tied up
with a rubber band. She had never seen a man with an earring and
such long hair. But then she had never known such cold, so much
rain. His silver earring was the strangeness of the West, another
culture-shock. She stared at it during classes, her eyes straying from
the white scribbles on the board. Most times she could hardly
understand anything. Only the notation was familiar. But how did
it all fit together? How did *this* formula lead to this? Her ignorance
and the impending exams were horrors she wanted to escape. His
long hair, a dull colour between yellow and brown, different
shades. It reminded her of a doll she had when she was young. She
had spent hours combing that doll's hair, stroking it. She had
longed for such straight hair. When she went to Paradise she
would have hair like that. When she ran it would fly behind her; if
she bent her head down it would fall over like silk and sweep the
flowers on the grass. She watched his pony-tail move as he wrote
and then looked up at the board. She pictured her doll, vivid
suddenly after years, and felt sick that she was day-dreaming in
class, not learning a thing.

The first days of term, when the classes started for the MSc in

Statistics, she was like someone tossed around by monstrous waves. Battered, as she lost her way to the different lecture rooms, fumbled with the photocopying machine, could not find anything in the library. She could scarcely hear or eat or see. Her eyes bulged with fright, watered from the cold. The course required a certain background, a background she didn't have. So she floundered, she and the other African students, the two Turkish girls, and the men from Brunei. Asafa, the short, round-faced Ethiopian, said, in his grave voice, as this collection from the Third World whispered their anxieties in grim Scottish corridors, the girls in nervous giggles, 'Last year, last year a Nigerian on this very same course committed suicide. *Cut his wrists.*'

Us and them, she thought. The ones who would do well, the ones who would crawl and sweat and barely pass. Two predetermined groups. Asafa, generous and wise (he was the oldest), leaned and whispered to Shadia, 'The Spanish girl is good. Very good.' His eyes bulged redder than Shadia's. He cushioned his fears every night in the university pub; she only cried. Their countries were next-door neighbours but he had never been to Sudan, and Shadia had never been to Ethiopia. 'But we meet in Aberdeen!', she had shrieked when this information was exchanged, giggling furiously. Collective fear had its euphoria.

'That boy Bryan,' said Asafa, 'is excellent.'

'The one with the earring?'

Asafa laughed and touched his own unadorned ear. 'The earring doesn't mean anything. He'll get the Distinction. He did his undergraduate here, got First Class Honours. That gives him an advantage. He knows all the lecturers, he knows the system.'

So the idea occurred to her of asking Bryan for the notes of his graduate year. If she strengthened her background in stochastic processes and time series, she would be better able to cope with the new material they were bombarded with every day. She watched him to judge if he was approachable. Next to the courteous Malaysian students, he was devoid of manners. He mumbled and slouched and did not speak with respect to the lecturers. He spoke to them as if they were his equals. And he did silly things. When he wanted to throw a piece of paper in the bin, he squashed it into a ball and from where he was sitting he aimed it at the bin. If he missed, he muttered under his breath. She thought that he was immature. But he was the only one who was sailing through the course.

The glossy handbook for overseas students had explained about the 'famous British reserve' and hinted that they should be grateful, things were worse further south, less 'hospitable'. In the cafeteria, drinking coffee with Asafa and the others, the picture of 'hospitable Scotland' was something different. Badr, the Malaysian, blinked and whispered, 'Yesterday our windows got smashed; my wife today is afraid to go out.'

'Thieves?' asked Shadia, her eyes wider than anyone else's.

'Racists,' said the Turkish girl, her lipstick chic, the word tripping out like silver, like ice.

Wisdom from Asafa, muted, before the collective silence, 'These people think they own the world . . .' and around them the aura of the dead Nigerian student. They were ashamed of that brother they had never seen. He had weakened, caved in. In the cafeteria, Bryan never sat with them. They never sat with him. He sat alone, sometimes reading the local paper. When Shadia walked in front of him he didn't smile. 'These people are strange . . . One day they greet you, the next day they don't . . .'

On Friday afternoon, as everyone was ready to leave the room after Linear Models, she gathered her courage and spoke to Bryan. He had spots on his chin and forehead, was taller than her, restless, as if he was in a hurry to go somewhere else. He put his calculator back in its case, his pen in his pocket. She asked him for his notes and his blue eyes behind his glasses took on the blankest look she had ever seen in her life. What was all the surprise for? Did he think she was an insect, was he surprised that she could speak?

A mumble for a reply, words strung together. So taken-aback, he was. He pushed his chair back under the table with his foot.

'Pardon?'

He slowed down, separated each word, 'Ah'll have them for ye on Monday.'

'Thank you.' She spoke English better than him! How pathetic. The whole of him was pathetic. He wore the same shirt every blessed day. Grey stripes and white.

On the weekends, Shadia never went out of the halls and unless someone telephoned long distance from home, she spoke to no one. There was time to remember Thursday nights in Khartoum, a wedding to go to with Fareed, driving in his red Mercedes. Or the club with her sisters. Sitting by the pool drinking lemonade with ice, the waiters all dressed in white. Sometimes people swam at night, dived in the water dark like the sky above. Here, in this country's weekend of Saturday and Sunday, Shadia washed her clothes and her hair. Her hair depressed her. The damp weather made it frizz up after she straightened it with hot tongs. So she had given up and now wore it in a bun all the time, tightly pulled back away from her face, the curls held down by pins and Vaseline Tonic. She didn't like this style, her corrugated hair, and in the mirror her eyes looked too large. The mirror in the public bathroom, at the end of the corridor to her room, had printed on it 'This is the face of someone with HIV.' She had written about this mirror to her sister, something foreign and sensational like hail and cars driving on the left. But she hadn't written that the mirror made her feel as if she had left her looks behind in Khartoum.

On the weekends, she made a list of the money she had spent, the sterling enough to keep a family alive back home. Yet she might fail her exams after all that expense, go back home empty-handed without a degree. Guilt was cold like the fog of this city. It came from everywhere. One day she forgot to pray in the morning. She reached the bus-stop and then realised that she hadn't prayed. That morning folded out like the nightmare she sometimes had, of discovering that she had gone out into the street without any clothes.

In the evening, when she was staring at multidimensional scaling, the telephone in the hall rang. She ran to answer it. Fareed's cheerful greeting. 'Here, Shadia, Mama and the girls want to speak to you.' His mother's endearments, 'They say it's so cold where you are . . .'

Shadia was engaged to Fareed. Fareed was a package that came with the 7Up franchise, the paper factory, the big house he was building, his sisters and widowed mother. Shadia was going to marry them all. She was going to be happy and make her mother happy. Her mother deserved happiness after the misfortunes of her life. A husband who left her for another woman. Six girls to bring up. People felt sorry for her mother. Six girls to educate and marry off. But your Lord is generous, each of the girls, it was often said, was lovelier than the other. They were clever too: dentist, pharmacist, architect, and all with the best of manners.

'We are just back from looking at the house,' Fareed's turn again to talk. 'It's coming along fine, they're putting the tiles down . . .'

'That's good, that's good,' her voice strange from not talking to anyone all day.

'The bathroom suites. If I get them all the same colour for us and the girls and Mama, I could get them on a discount. Blue, the girls are in favour of blue,' his voice echoed from one continent to another. Miles and miles.

'Blue is nice. Yes, better get them all the same colour.' He was building a block of flats, not a house. The ground-floor flat for his mother and the girls until they married, the first floor for him and Shadia. The girls' flats on the two top floors would be rented out.

When Shadia had first got engaged to Fareed, he was the son of a rich man. A man with the franchise for 7Up and the paper factory which had a monopoly in ladies' sanitary towels. Fareed's sisters never had to buy sanitary towels; their house was abundant with boxes of *Pinky*, fresh from the production line. But Fareed's father died of an unexpected heart attack soon after the engagement party (500 guests at the Hilton). Now Shadia was going to marry the rich man himself. You are a lucky, lucky girl, her mother said, and Shadia rubbed soap in her eyes so that Fareed would think she had been weeping his father's death.

There was no time to talk about her course on the telephone, no space for her anxieties. Fareed was not interested in her studies. He had said, 'I am very broad-minded to allow you to study abroad. Other men would not have put up with this . . .' It was her mother who was keen for her to study, to get a post-graduate degree from Britain and then have a career after she got married. 'This way,' her mother had said, 'you will have your in-laws' respect. They have money but you will have a degree. Don't end up like me. I left my education to marry your father and now . . .' Many conversations ended with her mother bitter, with her mother saying, 'No one suffers like I suffer,' and making Shadia droop. At night her mother sobbed in her sleep, noises that woke Shadia and her sisters.

No, on the long-distance line, there was no space for her worries. Talk about the Scottish weather. Picture Fareed, generously perspiring, his stomach straining the buttons of his shirt. Often she had nagged him to lose weight with no success. His mother's food was too good; his sisters were both overweight. On the long-distance line, listen to the Khartoum gossip as if listening to a radio play.

On Monday, without saying anything, Bryan slid two folders across the table towards her as if he did not want to come near her, did not want to talk to her. She wanted to say, 'I won't take them till you hand them to me politely.' But smarting, she said, 'Thank you very much.' *She* had manners. *She* was well brought up.

Back in her room, at her desk, the clearest handwriting she had ever seen. Sparse on the pages, clean. Clear and rounded like a child's, the tidiest notes. She cried over them, wept for no reason. She cried until she wetted one of the pages, stained the ink, blurred one of the formulas. She dabbed at it with a tissue but the paper flaked and became transparent. Should she apologise about the stain, say that she was drinking water, say that it was rain? Or should she just keep quiet, hope he wouldn't notice? She chided herself for all that concern. *He* wasn't concerned about wearing the same shirt every day. She was giving him too much attention thinking about him. He was just an immature and closed-in sort of character. He probably came from a small town; his parents were probably poor, low class. In Khartoum, she never mixed with people like that. Her mother liked her to be friends with people who were higher up. How else was she and her sisters going to marry well? She must study the notes and stop crying over this boy's handwriting. His handwriting had nothing to do with her, nothing to do with her at all.

Understanding after not understanding is fog lifting, is pictures swinging into focus, missing pieces slotting into place. It is fragments gelling, a sound vivid whole, a basis to build on. His notes were the knowledge she needed, the gaps. She struggled through them, not skimming them with the carelessness of incomprehension, but taking them in, making them a part of her, until in the depth of concentration, in the late hours of the nights, she lost awareness of time and place and at last when she slept she became epsilon and gamma and she became a variable making her way through discrete space from state i to state j.

It felt natural to talk to him. As if now that she had spent hours and days with his handwriting, she knew him in some way. She forgot the offence she had taken when he had slid his folders across the table to her, all the times he didn't say hello.

In the computer room, at the end of the statistical packages class, she went to him and said, 'Thanks for the notes. They are really good. I think I might not fail, after all. I might have a chance to pass.' Her eyes were dry from all the nights she had stayed up. She was tired and grateful.

He nodded and they spoke a little about the Poisson distribution, queuing theory. Everything was clear in his mind, his brain was a clear pane of glass where all the concepts were written out boldly and neatly. Today, he seemed more at ease talking to her, though he still shifted about from foot to foot, avoided her eyes.

He said, 'Do ye want to go for a coffee?'

She looked up at him. He was tall and she was not used to speaking to people with blue eyes. Then she made a mistake. Perhaps because she had been up late last night, she made that mistake. Perhaps there were other reasons for that mistake. The mistake of shifting from one level to another.

She said, 'I don't like your earring.'

The expression in his eyes, a focusing, no longer shifting away. He lifted his hand to his ear and tugged the earring off. His earlobe without the silver looked red and scarred.

She giggled because she was afraid, because he wasn't smiling, wasn't saying anything. She covered her mouth with her hand then wiped her forehead and eyes. A mistake was made and it was too late to go back. She plunged ahead, careless now, reckless, 'I don't like your long hair.'

He turned and walked away.

The next morning, Multivariate Analysis, and she came in late, dishevelled from running and the rain. The professor whose name she wasn't sure of (there were three who were Mc something) smiled unperturbed. All the lecturers were relaxed and urbane, in tweed jackets and polished shoes. Sometimes she wondered how the incoherent Bryan, if he did pursue an academic career, was going to transform himself into a professor like that. But it was none of her business.

Like most of the other students, she sat in the same seat in every class. Bryan sat a row ahead which was why she could always look at his hair. But he had cut it, there was no pony-tail today! Just his neck and the collar of the grey- and white-striped shirt.

Notes to take down. *In discriminant analysis, a linear combination of variables serves as the basis for assigning cases to groups . . .*

She was made up of layers. Somewhere inside, deep inside, under the crust of vanity, in the untampered-with essence, she would glow and be in awe, and be humble and think, this is just for me, he cut his hair for me. But there were other layers, bolder, more to the surface. Giggling. Wanting to catch hold of a friend. Guess what? You wouldn't *believe* what this idiot did!

Find a weighted average of variables . . . The weights are estimated so that they result in the best separation between the groups.

After the class he came over and said very seriously, without a smile. 'Ah've cut my hair.'

A part of her hollered with laughter, sang, you stupid boy, you stupid boy, I can see that, can't I?

She said, 'It looks nice.' She said the wrong thing and her face felt hot and she made herself look away so that she would not know his reaction. It was true though, he did look nice, he looked decent now.

She should have said to Bryan, when they first held their coffee mugs in their hands and were searching for an empty table, 'Let's sit with Asafa and the others.' Mistakes follow mistakes. Across the cafeteria, the Turkish girl saw them together and raised her perfect eyebrows; Badr met Shadia's eyes and quickly looked away. Shadia looked at Bryan and he was different, different without the earring and the pony-tail, transformed in some way. If he would put lemon juice on his spots . . . but it was none of her business. Maybe the boys who smashed Badr's windows looked like Bryan, but with fiercer eyes, no glasses. She must push him away from her. She must make him dislike her.

He asked her where she came from and when she replied, he said, 'Where's that?'

'Africa,' with sarcasm. 'Do you know where *that* is?'

His nose and cheeks under the rim of his glasses went red. Good, she thought, good. He will leave me now in peace.

He said, 'Ah know Sudan is in Africa; I meant where exactly in Africa.'

'North-east, south of Egypt. Where are *you* from?'

'Peterhead. It's north of here. By the sea.'

It was hard to believe that there was anything north of Aberdeen. It seemed to her that they were on the northern-most corner of the world. She knew better now than to imagine sun-tanning and sandy beaches for his 'by the sea'. More likely dismal skies, pale bad-tempered people shivering on the rocky shore.

'Your father works in Peterhead?'

'Aye, he does.'

She had grown up listening to the proper English of the BBC World Service only to come to Britain and find people saying 'yes' like it was said back home in Arabic, *aye*.

'What does he do, your father?'

He looked surprised, his blue eyes surprised, 'Ma' dad's a joiner.'

Fareed hired people like that to work on the house. Ordered them about.

'And your mother?' she asked.

He paused a little, stirred sugar in his coffee with a plastic spoon. 'She's a lollipop lady.'

Shadia smirked into her coffee, took a sip.

'My father,' she said proudly, 'is a doctor, a specialist.' Her father was a gynaecologist. The woman who was his wife now had been one of his patients. Before that, Shadia's friends had teased her about her father's job, crude jokes that made her laugh. It was all so sordid now.

'And my mother,' she blew the truth up out of proportion, 'comes from a very big family. A ruling family. If you British hadn't colonised us, my mother would have been a princess now.'

'Ye walk like a princess,' he said.

What a gullible, silly boy! She wiped her forehead with her hand, said, 'You mean I am conceited and proud?'

'No, Ah didnae mean that, no . . .' The packet of sugar he was tearing open tipped from his hand, its contents scattered over the table. 'Ah shit . . . sorry . . .' He tried to scoop up the sugar and knocked against his coffee mug, spilling a little on the table.

She took out a tissue from her bag, reached over and mopped up the stain. It was easy to pick up all the bits of sugar with the damp tissue.

'Thanks,' he mumbled and they were silent. The cafeteria was busy, full of the humming, buzzing sound of people talking to each other, trays and dishes. In Khartoum, she avoided being alone with Fareed. She preferred it when they were with others: their families, their many mutual friends. If they were ever alone, she imagined that her mother or her sister was with them, could hear them, and spoke to Fareed with that audience in mind.

Bryan was speaking to her, saying something about rowing on the river Dee. He went rowing on the weekends, he belonged to a rowing club.

To make herself pleasing to people was a skill Shadia was trained in. It was not difficult to please people. Agree with them, never dominate the conversation, be economical with the truth. Now here was someone whom all these rules needn't apply to.

She said to him, 'The Nile is superior to the Dee. I saw your

Dee, it is nothing, it is like a stream. There are two Niles, the Blue and the White, named after their colours. They come from the south, from two different places. They travel for miles over countries with different names, never knowing they will meet. I think they get tired of running alone, it is such a long way to the sea. They want to reach the sea so that they can rest, stop running. There is a bridge in Khartoum and under this bridge the two Niles meet and if you stand on the bridge and look down you can see the two waters mixing together.'

'Do ye get homesick?' he asked and she felt tired now, all this talk of the river running to rest in the sea. She had never talked like that before. Luxury words, and the question he asked.

'Things I should miss I don't miss. Instead I miss things I didn't think I would miss. The azan, the Muslim call to prayer from the mosque, I don't know if you know about it. I miss that. At dawn it used to wake me up. I would hear *prayer is better than sleep* and just go back to sleep, I never got up to pray.' She looked down at her hands on the table. There was no relief in confessions, only his smile, young, and something like wonder in his eyes.

'We did Islam in school,' he said. 'Ah went on a trip to Mecca.' He opened out his palms on the table.

'What!'

'In a book.'

'Oh.'

The coffee was finished. They should go now. She should go to the library before the next lecture and photocopy previous exam papers. Asafa, full of helpful advice, had shown her where to find them.

'What is your religion?' she asked.

'Dunno, nothing I suppose.'

'That's terrible! That's really terrible!' Her voice was too loud, concerned.

His face went red again and he tapped his spoon against the empty mug.

Waive all politeness, make him dislike her. Badr had said, even before his windows got smashed, that here in the West they hate Islam. Standing up to go, she said flippantly, 'Why don't you become a Muslim then?'

He shrugged, 'Ah wouldnae mind travelling to Mecca; I was keen on that book.'

Her eyes filled with tears. They blurred his face when he stood up. In the West they hate Islam and he . . . She said, 'Thanks for the coffee' and walked away but he followed her.

'Shadiya, Shadiya,' he pronounced her name wrong, three syllables instead of two, 'there's this museum about Africa. I've never been before. If you'd care to go, tomorrow . . .'

No sleep for the guilty, no rest, she should have said no, I can't go, no I have too much catching up to do. No sleep for the guilty, the memories come from another continent. Her father's new wife, happier than her mother, fewer worries. When Shadia visits she offers fruit in a glass bowl, icy oranges and guava, soothing in the heat. Shadia's father hadn't wanted a divorce, hadn't wanted to leave them, he wanted two wives not a divorce. But her mother had too much pride, she came from fading money, a family with a 'name'. Of the new wife her mother says, bitch, whore, the dregs of the earth, a nobody.

Tomorrow, she need not show up at the museum, even though she said that she would. She should have told Bryan she was engaged to be married, mentioned it casually. What did he expect from her? Europeans had different rules, reduced, abrupt customs. If Fareed knew about this . . . her secret thoughts like snakes . . . Perhaps she was like her father, a traitor. Her mother said that her father was devious. Sometimes Shadia was devious. With Fareed in the car, she would deliberately say, 'I need to stop at the grocer; we need things at home.' At the grocer he would pay for all her shopping and she would say, 'No, you shouldn't do that, no, you are too generous, you are embarrassing me.' With the money she saved, she would buy a blouse for her mother, nail varnish for her mother, a magazine, imported apples.

It was strange to leave her desk, lock her room and go out on a Saturday. In the hall the telephone rang. It was Fareed. If he knew where she was going now . . . Guilt was a like a hard-boiled egg stuck in her chest. A large cold egg.

'Shadia, I want you to buy some of the fixtures for the bathrooms. Taps and towel hangers. I'm going to send you a list of what I want exactly and the money . . .'

'I can't, I can't.'

'What do you mean you can't? If you go into any large department store . . .'

'I can't. I wouldn't know where to put these things, how to send them.'

There was a rustle on the line and she could hear someone whispering, Fareed distracted a little. He would be at work this time in the day, glass bottles filling up with clear effervescent, the words 7Up written in English and Arabic, white against the dark green.

'You can get good things, things that aren't available here. Gold would be good. It would match . . .'

Gold. Gold toilet seats!

'People are going to burn in Hell for eating out of gold dishes; you want to sit on gold!'

He laughed. He was used to getting his own way, not easily threatened, 'Are you joking with me?'

'No.'

In a quieter voice, 'This call is costing . . .'

She knew, she knew. He shouldn't have let her go away. She was not coping with the whole thing, she was not handling the stress. Like the Nigerian student.

'Shadia, gold-coloured, not gold. It's smart.'

'Allah is going to punish us for this; it's not right . . .'

'Since when have you become so religious!'

Bryan was waiting for her on the steps of the museum, familiar-looking against the strange grey of the city, streets where cars had their headlamps on in the middle of the afternoon. He wore a different shirt, a navy-blue jacket. He said, not looking at her, 'Ah was beginning to think you wouldnae turn up.'

There was no entry fee to the museum, no attendant handing out tickets. Bryan and Shadia walked on soft carpets, thick blue carpets that made Shadia want to take off her shoes. The first thing they saw was a Scottish man from Victorian times. He sat on a chair surrounded with possessions from Africa, over-flowing trunks, an ancient map strewn on the floor of the glass cabinet. All the light in the room came from this and other glass cabinets, gleamed on the wax. Shadia turned away, there was an ugliness in the life-like wispiness of his hair, his determined expression, the way he sat. A hero who had gone away and come back, laden, ready to report.

Bryan began to conscientiously study every display cabinet, read the posters on the wall. She followed him around and thought that he was studious, careful and studious, that was why he did so well in his degree. She watched the intent expression on his face as he looked at everything. For her the posters were an effort to read, the information difficult to take in. It had been so long since she had read anything outside the requirements of the course. But she persevered, saying the words to herself, moving her lips . . . *During the 18th and 19th centuries, north-east Scotland made a disproportionate impact on the world at large by contributing so many skilled and committed individuals . . . In serving an empire they gave and received, changed others and were themselves changed and often returned home with tangible reminders of their experiences.*

The tangible reminders were there to see, preserved in spite of the years. Her eyes skimmed over the disconnected objects out of place and time. Iron and copper, little statues. Nothing was of her, nothing belonged to her life at home, what she missed. Here was Europe's vision, the clichés about Africa: cold and old.

She had not expected the dim light and the hushed silence. Apart from Shadia and Bryan, there was only a man with a briefcase, a lady who took down notes, unless there were others out of sight on the second floor. Something electrical, the heating or the lights, gave out a humming sound like that of an air-conditioner. It made Shadia feel as if they were in an aeroplane without windows, detached from the world outside.

'He looks like you, don't you think?' she said to Bryan. They stood in front of a portrait of a soldier who died in the first year of this century. It was the colour of his eyes and his hair. But Bryan did not answer her, did not agree with her. He was preoccupied with reading the caption. When she looked at the portrait again, she saw that she was mistaken. That strength in the eyes, the purpose, was something Bryan didn't have. They had strong faith in those days long ago.

Biographies of explorers who were educated in Edinburgh; doctors, courage, they knew what to take to Africa: Christianity, commerce, civilisation. They knew what they wanted to bring back; cotton watered by the Blue Nile, the Zambezi river. She walked after Bryan, felt his concentration, his interest in what was before him and thought, 'In a photograph we would not look nice together.'

She touched the glass of a cabinet showing papyrus rolls, copper pots. She pressed her forehead and nose against the cool glass. If she could enter the cabinet, she would not make a good exhibit. She wasn't right, she was too modern, too full of mathematics.

Only the carpet, its petroleum blue, pleased her. She had come to this museum expecting sunlight and photographs of the Nile, something to appease her homesickness, a comfort, a message. But the messages were not for her, not for anyone like her. A letter from West Africa, 1762, an employee to his employer in Scotland. An employee trading European goods for African curiosities. *It was great difficulty to make the natives understand my meaning, even by an interpreter, it being a thing so seldom asked of them, but they have all undertaken to bring something and laughed heartily at me and said, I was a good man to love their country so much . . .*

Love my country so much. She should not be here; there was nothing for her here. She wanted to see minarets, boats fragile on the Nile, people. People like her father. Times she had sat in the waiting room of his clinic, among pregnant women, the pain in her heart because she was going to see him in a few minutes. His room, the air-conditioner and the smell of his pipe, his white coat. When she hugged him, he smelled of Listerine Mouthwash. He could never remember how old she was, what she was studying. Six daughters, how could he keep track? In his confusion, there was freedom for her, games to play, a lot of teasing. She visited his clinic in secret, telling lies to her mother. She loved him more than she loved her mother. Her mother who did everything for her, tidied her room, sewed her clothes from *Burda* magazine. Shadia was twenty-five and her mother washed everything for her by hand, even her pants and bras.

'I know why they went away,' said Bryan. 'I understand why they travelled.' At last he was talking. She had not seen him intense before. He spoke in a low voice, 'They had to get away, to leave here . . .'

'To escape from the horrible weather . . .' she was making fun of him. She wanted to put him down. The imperialists who had humiliated her history were heroes in his eyes.

He looked at her. 'To escape . . .' he repeated.

'They went to benefit themselves,' she said. 'People go away because they benefit in some way . . .'

'I want to get away,' he said.

She remembered when he had opened his palms on the table and said, 'I went on a trip to Mecca.' There had been pride in his voice.

'I should have gone somewhere else for the course,' he went on. 'A new place, somewhere down south.'

He was on a plateau, not like her. She was punching and struggling for a piece of paper that would say she was awarded an MSc from a British university. For him the course was a continuation.

'Come and see,' he said, and he held her arm. No one had touched her before, not since she had hugged her mother goodbye. Months now in this country and no one had touched her.

She pulled her arm away. She walked away, quickly up the stairs. Metal steps rattled under her feet. She ran up the stairs to the next floor. Guns, a row of guns aiming at her. They had been waiting to blow her away. Scottish arms of centuries ago, gun-fire in service of the empire.

Silver muzzles, a dirty grey now. They must have shone pretty once, under a sun far away. If they blew her away now, where would she fly and fall? A window that looked out at the hostile sky. She shivered in spite of the wool she was wearing, layers of clothes. Hell is not only blazing fire, a part of it is freezing cold, torturous ice and snow. In Scotland's winter you live a glimpse of this unseen world, feel the breath of it in your bones.

There was a bench and she sat down. There was no one here on this floor. She was alone with sketches of jungle animals, words on the wall. A diplomat away from home, in Ethiopia in 1903, Asafa's country long before Asafa was born. *It is difficult to imagine anything more satisfactory or better worth taking part in than a lion drive. We rode back to camp feeling very well indeed. Archie was quite right when he said that this was the first time since we have started that we have really been in Africa – the real Africa of jungle*

inhabited only by game, and plains where herds of antelope meet your
eye in every direction.

'Shadiya, don't cry.' He still pronounced her name wrong
because she had not shown him how to say it properly.

He sat next to her on the bench, the blur of his navy jacket
blocking the guns, the wall-length pattern of antelope herds. She
should explain that she cried easily; there was no need for the
alarm on his face. His awkward voice, 'Why are ye crying?' He
didn't know, he didn't understand. He was all wrong, not a
substitute . . .

'They are telling you lies in this museum,' she said. 'Don't
believe them. It's all wrong. It's not jungles and antelopes, it's
people. We have things like computers and cars. We have 7Up in
Africa and some people, a few people, have bathrooms with golden
taps . . . I shouldn't be here with you. You shouldn't talk to me . . .'

He said, 'Museums change; I can change . . .'

He didn't know it was a steep path she had no strength for. He
didn't understand. Many things, years and landscapes, gulfs. If she
was strong she would have explained and not tired of explaining.
She would have patiently taught him another language, letters
curved like the epsilon and gamma he knew from mathematics.
She would have showed him that words could be read from right
to left. If she was not small in the museum, if she was really strong,
she would have made his trip to Mecca real, not only in a book.

Majed

'What are you doing?' Hamid couldn't see her properly because he didn't have his glasses on. She was blurred over the kitchen sink, holding the bottle in her hand. She was not supposed to be holding that bottle. How did she get hold of it? He had hidden it behind the videos late last night, behind *Enter the Dragon*. He had washed his glass carefully over the kitchen sink, gargled with ASDA Protect then crept into bed beside her, careful, very careful not to wake her or the two youngest ones. Majed slept in the cot in the corner of the room, the newborn baby slept with them in the double bed so that Ruqiyyah could feed her during the night. During the night when Hamid had to go to the toilet he tried to be careful not to wake them up. Though sometimes he did, bumping into Majed's cot, stumbling on a toy. One night he had found himself, almost too late, not in the toilet but surrounded by the shoes that littered the entrance to the flat. He was startled into full consciousness by the baby crying.

'Ruqiyyah, what are you doing?' He should make a lunge at her, stop her before it was too late. It was precious stuff she was threatening to pour down the drain. But the whole household was in his way. A pile of washing waiting to go into the washing machine, the baby, sunk down and small, in her seat on the floor.

She was creamy and delicate, wearing tiny gloves so that she would not scratch herself. The kitchen table was in his way. Majed sat on his high chair covered in porridge, singing, banging the table with his spoon; Sarah talked to him and chewed toast. Robin scooped Rice Krispies into his mouth while staring at the box; Snap, Crackle and Pop flying and things you could send for if your parents gave you the money.

Ruqiyyah put the bottle down. But only because there were plates and baby bottles in the sink. She started to wash them up, water splashing everywhere.

She looked at Hamid and shook her head.

Hamid groaned. He was relieved he couldn't see her eyes, her blue eyes filled with tears maybe. She had not always been Ruqiyyah, she once was someone else with an ordinary name, a name a girl behind the counter in the Bank of Scotland might have. When she became Muslim she changed her name then left her husband. Robin and Sarah were not Hamid's children. Ruqiyyah had told Hamid horror stories about her previous marriage. She had left little out. When she went on about her ex-husband, Hamid felt shattered. He had never met Gavin (who wanted nothing to do with Ruqiyyah, Robin and Sarah and had never so much as sent them a bean), but that man stalked Hamid's nightmares. Among Hamid's many fears, was the fear of Gavin storming the flat, shaking him until his glasses fell off, 'You filthy nigger, *stay away* from my family.'

'Ruqiyyah, wait, I'll get my glasses.' He looked at the children. He looked back at her, made a face. When the children finished their breakfast and headed towards Children's TV, they could talk. They couldn't talk in front of Robin. He was old enough to understand, pick up things. He was sensitive. Hamid ruffled Robin's hair, said something jolly about Snap, Crackle and Pop. Robin smiled and this encouraged Hamid to be more jocular. Whenever Hamid was stressed, he changed into a clown. The hahaha of laughter covered problems. Hahaha had wheels, it was a skateboard to slide and escape on.

'I'll get my glasses.' He stumbled away. He needed the glasses. The glasses would give him confidence. He would be able to talk, explain. She was so good, so strong, because she was a convert. But he, he had been a Muslim all his life and was, it had to be said, relaxed about the whole thing. Wrong, yes it was wrong. He wasn't going to argue about that. Not with Ruqiyyah. Instead he would say . . . he would explain, that on the scale . . . yes on the scale (he was a scientist after all and understood scales), on the scale of all the forbidden things, it was not really so wrong, so bad. There were worse, much worse, the heavies, the Big Ones: black magic, adultery, abusing your parents (something the dreadful Gavin had done – *pushed the old dear round her living room* – may he rot in Hell on account of this for all eternity and more). Hamid would explain . . . Once he put his glasses on and the world cleared up he would explain. Human weakness etc., and Allah is all forgiving. That's right. Then a sad, comic face. A gentle hahaha. But she could counter that argument about forgiveness though. He must be careful. She would say that one has to repent first before one could be forgiven. And she would be right. Of course. Absolutely. He had every intention to repent. *Every* intention. But not now, not this minute, not today. A few more days, when he got himself sorted out, when this bottle was finished, when finished his PhD, when he got a proper job and did not need to work evenings in ASDA.

He found his glasses near the bed between the baby lotion and the zinc and castor oil. He put them on and felt better, more focused, more in control. Ruqiyyah hadn't yet dealt with this room. There were nappies on the floor, folded up and heavy. She had, though, stripped the sheets off Majed's cot. There were soft cartoon characters on the plastic mattress. Hamid rescued the prayer mat off the nappy-covered floor and dropped it on the unmade bed. He opened the window for the smells in the room to go out and fresh air to come in. Outside was another grey day, brown leaves all over the pavements. A gush of rainy air, a moment of contemplation. *Subhan Allah*, who would have ever thought that he, Hamid, born and bred on the banks of the Blue Nile, would end up here with a Scottish wife, who was a better Muslim than he was. Why had he married her? Because of the residence visa, to solve his problem with the Home Office once and for all. A friend had approached him once after Friday prayers (he did sometimes go to the mosque for Friday prayers, he was not *so* useless), and told him about Ruqiyyah, how she was a new convert with two little ones, how she needed a husband to take care of her. And you Hamid, need a visa . . . Why not? Why not? Ha ha. Is she pretty? Ha ha. There had been a time in Hamid's life when the only white people he saw were on the cinema screen, now they would be under one roof. Why not? He brushed his teeth with enthusiasm, sprayed himself with Old Spice, armed himself with the jolly laugh and set out to meet the three of them. Robin's shy face, the gaze of a child once bitten twice shy. A woman of average height, with bright anxious blue eyes, her hair covered with a black scarf, very conservatively dressed, no make-up. He breathed a sigh of relief that she was not lean like European women tended to be. Instead she was soft like his own faraway mother, like a girl he had once longed for in the University of Khartoum, a girl who had been unattainable. And if on that first meeting, Ruqiyyah's charms were deliberately hidden, they were obvious in her one-year-old daughter. Sarah was all smiles and wavy yellow hair, stretching out her arms, wanting to be carried, wanting to be noticed. After the awkwardness of their first meeting, a lot of hahaha, tantrums from Robin, desperate jokes, Hamid stopped laughing. He entered that steady place under laughter. He fell in love with the three of them, their pale needy faces, the fires that were repressed in them. His need for a visa, her need for security, no longer seemed grasping or callous. They were swept along by the children, his own children coming along, tumbling out soon, easily. Two years ago Majed, three weeks ago the baby. At school when Ruqiyyah and Majed went to pick up Robin, no one believed that they were brothers. Ruqiyyah with her children: two Europeans, two Africans. The other mothers outside the school looked at her oddly, smiled too politely. But Ruqiyyah could handle the other mothers, she had been through much worse. She had once escaped Gavin to a Women's Refuge, lived with rats and Robin having a child's equivalent of a nervous breakdown.

He must make it to the kitchen before she poured the Johnny Walker down the sink. He was angry. His secret was out and now that it was out it could not go back in again. It wasn't fair. If she was suspicious why hadn't she turned a blind eye, why had she searched for the proof? It wasn't fair. These were his private moments, late at night, all by himself, the children asleep, Ruqiyyah asleep. The whole soft sofa to himself, a glass of whisky in his hand, the television purring sights that held his attention, kung fu, football, Sumo wrestling, Prince Naseem thrashing someone. Anything that blocked out the thesis, the humiliating hours spent mopping up ASDA's floor, the demanding, roving kids. Anything cheerful, not the news, definitely not the news. The last thing he wanted at that time of night were his brothers and sisters suffering in the West Bank. His own warm, private moments, the little man on the bottle of Johnny Walker. That little man was Johnny, an average sort of guy and because he was walking, striding along with his top hat, he was a Walker, Johnny Walker. Or perhaps because he *was* Johnny Walker, he was represented as walking, striding along happily. It was interesting, but at the end it didn't matter and that was what Hamid wanted at that time of night. Things that didn't matter. At times he took his glasses off, let the television become a blur, and he would become a blur too, a hazy, warm, lovable blur. Nothing sharp, nothing definite. The exact number of years he had been a PhD student. Don't count, man, don't count. Laughter blurred things too. Hahaha. His thesis was not going to make it. He must, his supervisor said, *stretch himself.* His thesis now, as it stood, was *not meaty enough.* There was a lot of meat in ASDA, shelves. When he cleaned underneath them, he shivered from the cold. Not meaty enough. Johnny Walker was slight and not at all meaty and he was alright, successful, striding along brimming with confidence. Why shouldn't a man with an unfinished thesis and an ego-bashing job at ASDA sit up late at night, once in a while, settle down in front of the television and sink in. Sink into the warmth of the whisky and the froth of the TV. Once in a while?

Majed lunged into the room. He squealed when he saw Hamid sitting on the bed. 'Majed, say salaam, shake hands.' Hamid held his hand out. Majed took his fist out of his mouth and placed it, covered in saliva, in his father's hand. Then he pointed to his cot, transformed because the sheet wasn't on it. It wasn't often that Ruqiyyah changed the sheets. Majed walked over to his cot mumbling exclamations of surprise. He put his hands through the bars and patted the cartoon characters on the plastic mattress. 'Mummy's washing your sheet. You'll be getting a nice clean sheet,' Hamid said. It was rare that the two of them were alone together. Hamid held him up and hugged him, put him on his lap. He loved him so much. He loved his smell and roundness, his tight little curls and wide forehead. Majed was a piece of him, a purer piece of him. And that love was a secret because it was not the same love he felt for Robin and Sarah. He feared for Majed, throat-catching fear, while with Sarah and Robin he was calm and sensible. He dreamt about Majed. Majed crushed under a bus and Hamid roaring from the pain, which came from deep inside, which surfaced into sobs, then Ruqiyyah's voice, her hand on his cheeks, what's wrong, what's the matter and the wave of shame with the silent coolness of waking up. I'm sorry, I'm sorry, it's nothing, go back to sleep. The more he loved Majed and the newborn baby, the kinder Hamid was to Robin and Sarah. He must not be unjust. Ruqiyyah must never feel that he favoured their children over Robin and Sarah. It was a rare, precious moment when he was alone with Majed, no one watching them. He threw him up in the air and Majed squealed and laughed. He stood Majed on the bed and let him run, jump, fly from the bed into his outstretched arms. Then he remembered Ruqiyyah in the kitchen. The memory dampened the fun. He sent Majed off to join Sarah and Robin in front of the television (already the blocked-nose voice of *Rugrats* filled the flat), and he walked back to the kitchen.

Ruqiyyah was clearing the things off the kitchen table; the baby was asleep in her chair on the floor. With his glasses on now, Hamid could clearly see the whisky bottle. Two-thirds empty, two-thirds . . . His heart sank, that much . . . or had she already poured some out? No. No, she hadn't. He knew what she was going to do. She was going to clear the kitchen, wash everything and put it away, then ceremoniously tip the bottle into the empty sink.

She started cleaning up Majed's high-chair. Her hair fell over her eyes. She wore an apron with Bugs Bunny on it. She was beautiful, not like women on TV, but with looks that would have been appreciated in another part of the world, in another century. Her lips were naturally red. He had thought, before they got married, that she was wearing lipstick. She wore hijab when she went out, she got up at dawn and prayed. This seriousness that he didn't have, baffled him. Something Scottish she brought with her when she stepped into Islam. The story of her conversion amazed him as much as her stories about Gavin shocked and sickened him. She had read books about Islam. Books Gavin had snatched and torn up. Not because they were about Islam, but because she was sitting on her fat arse reading instead of doing what he wanted her to do.

She wanted to learn Arabic. Hamid would doze in bed and next to him she would hold *Simple Words in Arabic*, over the head of the baby she was feeding. 'How do you say this?' she would ask from time to time, nudging him awake. When Hamid read Qur'an out loud (he went through religious spells in Ramadan and whenever one of the children fell ill), she said, 'I wish I could read like you.'

He started to help her tidy up. He closed the flaps on the box of Rice Krispies, put it away in the cupboard. When she finished wiping the table and started on the floor, he lifted up the baby's seat and put it on the table. If she would talk to him, shout at him it would be better. Instead he was getting this silent treatment. He began to feel impatient. What had made her search for the bottle? A smell . . . ?

Attack is the best form of defence. Laughter blurs things, smoothes them over. Hahaha. He began to talk, he put on his most endearing voice, tried a joke. Hahaha. She didn't answer him, didn't smile. She pushed her hair away from her face, poured powder into the drawer of the washing machine. She bent down and began to load the washing into the machine. It was linen, the sheets that had been on Majed's cot. Hamid said, 'But how did you know? Tell me.'

She sat on her heels, closed the door of the washing machine. She said, 'You pissed in Majed's cot. You thought you were in the toilet.' She twisted the dial that started the wash cycle, 'I pretended to be asleep. He didn't wake up.'

There is a place under laughter, under the hahaha.

Hamid saw her stand up, pick up the Johnny Walker and pour what was left of it down the drain. She poured it carefully so that not a single drop splashed on the sink where later the children's bowls and bottles would wait to be washed.

Baby Love

We were going to the Hilton. I wasn't sure whether to wear my denim skirt or a dress. Better wear a dress, my pink one with the belt. I liked belts – that's what I liked about my school uniform, its white belt. My dress needed ironing so I had to open the kitchen window and shout for Ali to do it. He must have been asleep because he took ages to answer. 'Hurry' I told him when he appeared. I still couldn't get used to seeing him without that lump on his eyebrow that was as big as a ping-pong ball. My father paid for the operation to remove it and Ali came back from the hospital smiling and very pleased with himself. Now he had higher aspirations and didn't want to be a houseboy any more. At the end of the month he was going to leave us and become an electrician.

I polished my nails Aubergine and remembered to clean my sandals. It was half past one, thirty-one minutes past one. She wouldn't, like Sameer, park and ring the doorbell. She would blow the car-horn and I mustn't rush out and seem too keen. Lunch at the Hilton, I was keen. It would be Open Buffet, eat as much as you like. But today with my future mother-in-law, I had no intention of eating as much as I liked. She would be shocked.

A car-horn. I leapt up from the sofa and checked my face again in the hall mirror. I shouted, 'Ali, I'm going!' and walked as slowly as I could down the garden path.

'Hi.' I couldn't call her Auntie because she didn't like it. Because she was African-American she wanted me to call her Janet, but it was so rude. So I didn't call her anything and whenever I spoke about her to Sameer I said 'your mom'.

'Hi, Majda. Just look at your pretty dress!' Her voice was rich and deep though she was delicately built, with slender arms. I loved the way she pronounced my name. I loved her American accent.

She drove fast, confident. When I asked about Uncle Kamal, who I could thankfully call Uncle, she said, 'He's having lunch with his sister . . . gobbledygook.' I laughed. She hated Sudanese food, except for kebab. She hated cumin and we put cumin in everything. The food she cooked was deliberate and slightly sweet. When she made salad she said, 'I threw together a salad.'

I rolled up the window so the wind wouldn't mess up my hair. I thought of the smooth, air-conditioned lobby of the Hilton, my sandals on the marbled floor, white tablecloths and napkins.

'Sam called last night,' she said.

'Oh, why didn't he call me too?' I sounded childish and envious.

'He said he tried you but you were out.'

'Ali is so stupid,' I said, 'I was at the neighbours' next door. He could have fetched me.'

'It's just as well he didn't, Majda. Long-distance calls are so expensive and you guys chat for so long, even though Sam's on a student budget.' She clicked on the indicator to turn left into Airport Road. It was a loud clicking noise, louder than any other car I've been in.

I went on, 'Ali just shouts "Out, out, they're all out!" and slams down the phone. We never know who called us . . .'

'Well, why don't you give Sam a call tonight?'

It's funny how she always Americanised his name and called

him Sam. He didn't mind, he never corrected her. 'Did he say he'd booked his ticket?'

She looked straight at the road. 'No, he didn't.'

'Maybe it's too early. Maybe he'll get his ticket in the next week or so.'

She didn't reply and the silence between us was odd. I remembered last night's dream and again felt queasy.

The first time Sameer took me to his house was wonderful. Of course I had seen Janet and Uncle Kamal before at the club, so it was the house that was new. There was a policeman at the gate because Uncle Kamal was now Minister of Agriculture and their garden was much neater than ours. But I was more interested in the inside of the house – the way it looked and the way it smelled and its coolness. The colours were different from our house, more purple and orange. Then there were the pictures on the wall. One was rude because you could see the woman's breasts. One was a large black and white photo of Uncle Kamal when he was a student in Chicago. He looked so serious and handsome in a suit and a hat – just like in an old film. Everything in the house was from America; the furniture and the videotapes. Even the drink Sameer gave me, he said it was called Kool-Aid. His room had a poster of Malcolm X who I didn't know and Bob Marley who I did. On his desk were a pile of chemistry textbooks and a photo of me. In the sitting room we watched an early *Soul Train* on which The Supremes sang 'Baby Love' while Janet flicked through the pages of *Ebony*. I loved that magazine when I looked at it. 'You can take it, I'm all done with it,' Janet said. I took *Ebony* with me to school and showed it off to my friends. We had never seen a magazine like that before. Girls who looked like us but were so glamorous, so obviously Western. I was proud of my future mother-in-law.

* * *

Janet turned the car left and we were suddenly bouncing down the dusty side street that led to the American Club. The club was at the end of the street; in front of it was a Christian cemetery. Janet parked facing the cemetery and I could see the headstones, a dusty statue of an angel. I felt confused. We were going to the Hilton. We couldn't be going to the cemetery. Maybe she was picking something up from the club? But she didn't say anything and got out of the car. I followed, trying to think of something to say that wouldn't be rude. I couldn't say, 'I thought we were going to the Hilton' because that would be critical and complaining. Maybe I had misunderstood. Maybe we were going to the Hilton later. Maybe she would say something now about why she had changed her mind. She didn't.

We walked up the concrete path that led to the swimming pool. To the left was the tennis court, which on Saturday nights became a cinema. I was over-dressed for the club; I should have worn my denim skirt. I felt subdued because of that and because the club was full of memories. Here was where I had met Sameer, and the first time he spoke to me, and the day he said, 'I dreamt of you last night', and the day I waited for him and he didn't come, and all the times we drank grapefruit juice and shared paper plates of French fries or sat by the pool, his voice normal and bored asking the waiter 'So what's the special today', and his voice different and nice when he looked at me and said, 'Majda, do you want a Sloppy Joe?' And the day he said, 'My mom and dad want me to go to college in the States', and the day I gave him my diary to read, and afternoons watching him play tennis and the day we had our biggest quarrel because he said, 'That skirt's transparent, don't wear it again.'

Janet chose a table by the pool. It was in the shade and she took off her sunglasses. She smiled at me and I smiled back, fighting disappointment. It was too late to mention the Hilton. Before she parked, I should have said innocently, 'I thought we were going to the Hilton!' Maybe I had misunderstood. My mother always tells me I only hear what I want to hear. I must have misunderstood Janet.

'Anyone that we know?' She scanned the pool and all the tables. I looked around too but my friends didn't come that time of day.

'There's Greta,' Janet said, nodding towards a large woman in a black swimsuit who was carefully coming out of the pool. Greta had big, beautiful blonde hair, cut short in a bob. Now it was a smooth wet sheet, clinging to her neck and shoulders. It made her head look small and her body huge.

Benjamin, the Southern waiter appeared. 'What will you have?' asked Janet. Unlike the Hilton there was no need for a menu here, we all knew it by heart.

'I don't know. What are you going to have?' I sounded sulky and felt ashamed. I sat up straight in my chair and opened my eyes wide so as to appear interested.

'What's the special?' she asked Benjamin.

'Chicken-in-the-basket.'

She raised her eyebrows. 'That sounds fun!'

I beamed back.

'Two specials, Benjamin,' she said, 'and I'll have an Iced Tea. Majda, what will you have to drink?'

'The same . . . Iced Tea,' I said, even though I hated it.

Benjamin went away and we were quiet listening to the sounds of the club, watching the few who were swimming. I could hear the children from over the high wall that separated the club from St Francis' Primary School. The last time Sameer was here on holiday, we sometimes used to be quiet too and listen to the sounds of the school. I'd say to him, 'Tell me about America, tell me about your university.' He was glad he had gone. At first it had been his parents' idea and he didn't want to leave me, but now he said that studying in Chicago was great.

He came back different, he had changed; become more soft and more hard at the same time. He said sometimes he felt ashamed he was half-Sudanese and he wanted to throw that side of him away. 'Can you imagine how it feels, to be made up of two parts, one the richest, most powerful country in the world and the other the poorest and weakest.' I said, 'You're just you, you're not made up of two parts. If you weren't genuinely Sudanese you wouldn't have got angry with me for wearing that see-through skirt.' He shrugged and said, 'That was last year, that was a long time ago.' So I wore it again, the day before he went back and he didn't complain.

'Janet!' It was Auntie Greta, making her way towards us in a billowing tie-dye dress, her damp hair combed away from her forehead. I stood up and kissed her. Her cheeks were cool and she smelt of chlorine.

'Having lunch with your future daughter-in-law!' She sat down and blocked my view of the pool.

'Did you enjoy your swim?' asked Janet.

'Oh yes. It's always nice and quiet this time of day.' Greta turned to me. 'And so when is the engagement party?'

I smiled. 'Next month, when Sameer comes for his holidays.' We were going to have a huge party at the Hilton, exchange rings, have a photographer, as well as a video recording. When I thought of Sameer wearing a suit and me in my new evening dress, my stomach tingled with excitement.

'I don't understand this Sudanese custom of having official engagements,' said Janet to Greta. 'Why can't they just date like kids do in the States? They're so young!'

Greta shrugged. 'It's a Sudanese custom, part of the Muslim culture.'

'I'm not that young,' I said. 'My mother was my age when she got married.'

They didn't say anything, just exchanged looks. For the first time it occurred to me that my mother was Sudanese and they were not, my mother was brought up as a Muslim and they were not.

'And when will you actually get married?' asked Greta.

This was a sore point. Sameer and I wanted to get married as soon as possible while both sets of parents insisted that he finish his studies first.

'Insha' Allah in a year or so,' I said. I wished people would stop asking me this question. It was more likely going to be in three years' time. It would be another decade then and anything could happen in between. Like last night's horrible dream: Sameer looking at me like I was nobody, like he couldn't remember me any more. Sameer telling me he'd met someone else, someone American and prettier than me. It could happen, couldn't it? Uncle Kamal had been engaged to his cousin and then he went to study in Chicago and met Janet. Greta's husband had gone to study in Poland and came home with Greta. Maybe Sameer would meet someone too. There were no guarantees – if Allah didn't want us to get married, we wouldn't get married. It would be like today, thinking and dressing for the Hilton, and ending up here.

'We're all looking forward to your wedding,' Greta said brightly.

I grimaced.

'Well, there's no hurry, they're still far too young,' said Janet. 'When they both graduate, insha' Allah.' She pronounced it as if it were all one word, *inshallah*. She said it in a way as if she was making fun.

Benjamin appeared with the Iced Teas and the chickens. He plonked a napkin in front of me that was more grey than white. The knife and fork had stains that I rubbed away with my fingers. Where was I now and where was the Hilton?

'Can you get me ketchup, please?' I said to Benjamin. The club made its own ketchup. It was cheaper than the imported Heinz and tasted more tomatoey.

'Have something, Greta.' Janet raised her hand to detain Benjamin.

'I'll just have a Pepsi.'

I ate my chicken and listened to them talk. Janet ate her chicken with her hand so I did too. I liked listening to them: all the foreign wives' gossip. Many of the American Club members were foreign wives married to Sudanese men. Many like Sameer had foreign mothers. I was a rare exception, one hundred percent Sudanese. For me foreignness was like a dress I put on, it was not in my blood. Greta didn't have any children. When Greta first came to Khartoum, she had lived next door to Janet and Janet had helped her settle in. Now Greta said something funny about diets and I laughed. Janet smiled and wiped her mouth with her napkin. She was so dainty next to her loud, hearty friend.

'I have something to show you,' said Greta, looking at me. 'This is me and Janet when I first came to Khartoum nineteen years ago. Look how thin I was!' From her handbag, she took out a black and white photo. She put it in front of me and Janet leaned over to look. In the photo Greta was unrecognisable, slim and with long flowing blonde hair. And Janet looked exactly like the most beautiful of the Supremes, her hair high on her head. She was holding Sameer on her lap. He was the most gorgeous, gorgeous baby; smiling and bald, dimpled and fat. I couldn't help it, it came out in a whine, 'Aah, I want to have a baby like that.'

'Not till my son graduates, honey,' said Janet, taking the photo away from me and giving it back to Greta. 'I'm in *no* hurry to be a grandma!'

I stared at the place on the table where the photo had been. Greta patted my arm. 'Insha' Allah you'll have lots of babies, Majda,' she said, her eyes soft and grey. She put the photo back in her handbag and said, 'Well, I'd better be off now.'

I watched her as she walked away, dwarfing Benjamin who

crossed her path. I said to Janet, 'Auntie Greta looked so beautiful when she was young.' It was as if I could still see the photograph.

'Those were really hard years for Greta,' Janet said, gesturing to Benjamin to get the bill. 'She kept having one miscarriage after the other. She went all the way to London and had all sorts of treatment with a doctor in Harley Street but it was no use. They're loaded but there are some things money can't buy.'

'Is there a way of being sure that when . . . if . . . whether someone can have a baby or not . . . ?'

'Not unless you start trying, no.'

'So maybe, just maybe,' I croaked, 'Sameer and I won't ever . . . ever be able to have any babies?'

'Oh for God's sake, Majda, let the future take care of itself!'

'I'm sorry,' I mumbled. It seemed the right thing to say because I had annoyed her and made her raise her voice.

'Look,' she said, her voice was low but her eyes shrewd and knowing. 'You're very young. You'll change as you get older, you'll see things differently. Maybe you'll even change your mind about Sam . . .'

'No, never,' I interrupted, but she went on.

'Or maybe you'll decide you don't want to get married at all.' She raised both her hands. 'There are all sorts of possibilities. Why, yesterday on the phone, Sam was saying he might not be able to make it to the engagement next month! He's changed, Majda, he's been thinking things over. Personally I think he's far too young to commit himself but that's something you two will have to talk over.'

I was again in my bad dream. The sick fear. He'd met someone else. Another girl, American and prettier than me.

She looked away from me, at the club. She sounded dreamy, like she was talking to herself. 'There are so many fresh opportunities for him there. To come back here, to tie himself to Sudan, would be a step backward.'

I strained to understand, to get it right this time, not to hear Hilton and end up in the American Club.

She looked at me and laughed. 'Oh, don't you dare start crying here in front of everyone!' She touched my cheek and made her voice sweet. 'Come on now, finish your drink and then I can drive you home.'

I gulped the rest of my Iced Tea and coughed. It was diluted and more horrible because of the melted ice.

Something Old, Something New

H er country disturbed him. It reminded him of the first time
he had held a human bone, the touching simplicity of it, the
strength. Such was the landscape of Khartoum; bone-coloured sky,
a purity in the desert air, bareness. A bit austere and therefore
static. But he was driven by feelings, that was why he was here,
that was why he had crossed boundaries and seas, and now walked
through a blaze of hot air from the aeroplane steps to the terminal.

She was waiting for him outside the airport, wearing national
dress, a pale orange tobe that made her appear even more slender
than she was. I mustn't kiss you. No, she laughed, you mustn't. He
had forgotten how vibrant she was, how happy she made him feel.
She talked, asked him questions. Did you have a good trip, are you
hungry, did all your luggage arrive, were they nice to you in
Customs, I missed you too. There was a catch in her voice when
she said that; in spite of her confidence she was shy. Come, come
and meet my brother. They began to walk across a car park that
was disorganised and dusty, the sun gleaming on the cars.

Her brother was leaning against a dilapidated Toyota. He was
lanky with a hard-done-by expression. He looked irritated. Perhaps
by the conflicting desire to get his sister off his hands and his
misgivings about her marrying a foreigner. How did he see him

now, through those narrow eyes, how did he judge him? A European coming to shake his hand, murmuring salaamu alleikum, predictably wearing jeans, a white shirt, but somewhat subdued for a foreigner.

She sat in the front next to her brother. He sat in the back with the rucksack that wouldn't fit in the boot. The car seats were shabby, a thin film of dust covered everything. I will get used to the dust, he told himself, but not the heat. He could do with a breath of fresh air, that tang of rain he was accustomed to. He wanted her to be next to him. And it suddenly seemed to him, in a peevish sort of way, unfair that they should be separated like that. She turned her head back and looked at him, smiled as if she knew. He wanted to say, you have no idea how much I ache for you, you have no idea. But he could not say that, not least because the brother understood English.

It was like a ride in a funfair. The windows wide open; voices, noises, car-horns, people crossing the road at random, pausing in the middle, touching the cars with their fingers as if the cars were benign cattle. Any one of these passers-by could easily punch him through the window, yank off his watch, his sunglasses, snatch his wallet from the pocket of his shirt. He tried to roll up the window but couldn't. She turned and said, it's broken, I'm sorry. Her calmness made him feel that he needn't be so nervous. A group of schoolboys walked on the pavement, one of them stared at him, grinned and waved. He became aware that everyone looked like her, shared her colour, the women were dressed like her and they walked with the same slowness which had seemed to him exotic when he had seen her walking in Edinburgh.

Everything is new for you; she turned and glanced at him gently. The brother said something in Arabic.

The car moved away from the crowded market to a wide shady road. Look, she said, take off your sunglasses and look. There's the Nile.

And there was the Nile, a blue he had never seen before, a child's blue, a dream's blue. Do you like it? she asked. She was proud of her Nile.

Yes, it's beautiful, he replied. But as he spoke he noticed that the river's flow was forceful, not innocent, not playful. Crocodiles no doubt lurked beneath the surface, hungry and ruthless. He could picture an accident; blood, death, bones.

And here is your hotel, she said. I booked you into the Hilton. She was proud that her country had a Hilton.

The car swept up the drive. A porter in a gaudy green uniform and stiff turban opened the door for him before he could do it himself. (In any case the car had been in an accident and the dented door could only be opened from outside). The porter took his rucksack; there was a small fuss involving the brother in order to open the boot and get the suitcase. His luggage was mostly presents for her family. She had told him on the phone what to get and how much to get. They would be offended, she had explained, if you come empty-handed, they would think you don't care for me enough.

The hotel lobby was impressive, the cool tingling blast of the air-conditioner, music playing, an expanse of marble. He felt soothed somehow, more in control after the bumpy ride. With the brother away to park the car and a queue at the reception desk, they suddenly had time to talk.

I need an exit visa, she explained, to be able to leave and go back with you. To get the exit visa, I have to give a reason for leaving the country.

Because you're my wife, he said and they smiled at the word. Will be my wife. Will be insha' Allah.

Insha' Allah.

That's it, she said, we won't be able to get married and just leave. We'll have to stay a few days till the papers get sorted out. And the British Embassy . . . that's another story.

I don't understand what the problem is, he said.

Oh, she sighed, people have a wedding and they go off on their honeymoon. But we won't be able to do that, we will have to hang around and run from the Ministry of Interior to the Passport office to the British Embassy.

I see, he said, I see. Do I need an exit visa?

No, you're a visitor, you can leave whenever you like. But I need a visa, I need a reason to leave.

Right.

They looked at each other and then he said, I don't think your brother likes me.

No, no, he doesn't mean to be unfriendly . . . you'll see.

The first time he saw her was at the Sudanese restaurant near the new mosque in Edinburgh. His old chemistry teacher had taken him there after Friday prayers. When she brought the menu, she said to them that the peanut soup was good, a speciality, but his teacher wanted the humus salad and he ordered the lentil soup instead because it was familiar. He was by nature cautious, wanting new things but held back by a vague mistrust. It was enough for the time being that he had stepped into the Nile Café, he had no intention of experimenting with weird tastes.

He was conscious of her footsteps as she came from the kitchen, up the stairs. She was wearing trousers and a brown headscarf that was tied at the back of her neck. She had very black eyes that slanted. After that day he went to the Nile Café alone and often. It was convenient, close to the Department of Zoology where he worked as a lab technician. He wondered if, as she leant and put the dish of couscous in front of him, she could smell the chemicals on him.

They got talking because there weren't many customers in the restaurant and she had time on her hands. The restaurant was new and word had not yet got round that it was good.

We've started to get a few people coming in from the mosque, she told him. Friday especially is a good day.

Yes, it was a Friday when I first came here and met you.

She smiled in a friendly way.

He told her that at one time he had not known that the big building next to the restaurant was a mosque. There was no sign that said so. I thought it was a church, he said, and she laughed and laughed. He left her an extra tip that day; it was not often that people laughed at his jokes.

Had it not been for his old chemistry teacher he would never have gone to the mosque. At a bus stop, a face he had not seen for a number of years. A face associated with a positive feeling, a time of encouragement. Secondary school, the ease with which he had written lab reports. They recognised each other straight away. How are you? What are you doing now? You were my best student.

In primary and secondary school, he had been the brightest in his class, the most able. He sat for the three sciences in his Standard Grades and got three As. It was the same when he did his Highers. There was no reason at all, his teachers said, why he should not sail through medical school. But he got to his third year in medicine and failed, failed again and dropped out. He had counselling and his parents were supportive, but no one really ever understood what had gone wrong. He was as bewildered by his failure as everyone else was. His get-up-and-go had suddenly disappeared, as if amputated. What's it all for, what's the point?, he asked himself. He asked himself the taboo questions. And really, that was the worst of it, these were the questions that brought all the walls down.

Snap out of it, he was told. And snap out of it he eventually did, a girlfriend helped but then she found a job in London and drifted away. He was simply not up to medical school. It's a shame, everyone agreed. They were sympathetic but at the same time they labelled him now, they put him in a box; a student who had 'dropped out', a 'giver-upper'.

One day when she brought him his plate of aubergine and mince meat he asked her, would you like to go up Arthur's Seat?

She had never been there before. It was windy, a summer wind that carried away the hats of tourists and messed up people's hair. Because her hair was covered, she looked neat, slightly apart from everyone else. It made the outing not as carefree as he imagined it would. She told him she had recently got divorced after six months of marriage. She laughed when she said six months not six years, but he could tell she was sore – it was in her eyes. You have beautiful eyes, he said.

Everyone tells me that, she replied. He flushed and looked away at the green and grey houses that made up Edinburgh. She had wanted to talk about her divorce, she had not wanted to hear compliments.

They talked a little about the castle. He told her about his girlfriend, not the nice one who had gone down south, but the previous one who had dumped him. He was able to laugh about it now.

She said her husband had married her against his will. Not against her will, she stressed, but his will. He was in love with an English girl but his family disapproved and stopped sending the money he needed to continue his studies in Edinburgh. They thought a Sudanese girl like her would make him forget the girlfriend he had been living with. They were wrong. Everything went wrong from day one. It's a stupid story, she said, her hands in her pockets.

Did you love him? he asked her. Yes, she had loved him, wanted to love him. She had not known about his English girlfriend. After the honeymoon, when he brought her to Edinburgh and started acting strange, she asked him and he told her everything.

Would you believe it, she said, his family now blame me for the divorce? They say I wasn't clever enough, I didn't try hard enough. They're going around Khartoum saying all these things about me. That's why I don't want to go back. But I'll have to eventually when my visa runs out.

I'm glad I'm not pregnant, she went on. I thank Allah every day that I didn't become pregnant.

After that they spoke about faith. He told her how he had become a Muslim. He spoke about his former chemistry teacher – after meeting again they had fallen back into the swing of their old teacher-student relationship. She listened, fascinated. She asked him questions. What was his religion before? He had been a Catholic. Has he always believed in God? Yes. Why on earth did he convert?

She seemed almost surprised by his answers. She associated Islam with her dark skin, her African blood, her own weakness. She couldn't really understand why anyone like him would want to join the wretched of the world. But he spoke with warmth. It made her look at him properly, as if for the first time. Your parents probably don't like it, she said, and your friends? They won't like you changing. She was candid in that way.

And she was right. He had lost one friend after a bitter, unnecessary argument, another withdrew. His parents struggled to hide their dismay. Ever since he had dropped out of medical school, they had feared for his well-being, fretted that he would get sucked up into unemployment, drugs, depression; the underworld that throbbed and dragged itself parallel to their active middle-class life. Only last week, their neighbours' son had hanged himself (drugs, of course, and days without showering). There was a secret plague that targeted young men.

Despite their misgiving about his conversion to Islam, his parents eventually had to admit that he looked well; he put on a bit of weight, got a raise at work. If only he would not talk about religion. They did not understand that side of him that was theoretical, intangible, belonging to the spiritual world. If only he would not mention religion then it would be easier to pretend that nothing had changed. He was confident enough to humour them. Elated that the questions he had once asked – what's it all for, what does it all mean, what's the point of going on? – the questions that had tilted the walls around him and nearly smothered him, were now valid. They were questions that had answers, answers that provoked other questions, that opened new doors, that urged him to look at things in another way, like holding a cube in his hand, turning it round and round, or like moving around a tall column and looking at it from the other side, how different it was and how the same.

When he took her to meet his parents, the afternoon was a huge success. We're going to get married, he said, and there was a kind of relief in his mother's eyes. It was easier for his parents to accept that he was in love with a Muslim girl than it was to accept that he was in love with Islam.

From the balcony of his hotel room, he looked out at the Blue Nile. Sunshine so bright that he saw strands of shimmering light. Palm trees, boats, the river was so blue. Would the water be cool, he wondered, or tepid? He felt sleepy. The phone rang and he went indoors again, sliding the tinted glass door behind him.

Her happy voice again. What were you doing, why aren't you asleep, everyone sleeps this time in the afternoon, it's siesta time, you must be exhausted. Did you remember to bring dollar bills – not sterling, not travellers' cheques? You mustn't eat at the hotel, it will be terribly expensive, you must eat only with us here at home. Yes, we'll pick you up later. You'll come for dinner, you'll meet my parents. Don't forget the gifts. Are you going to dream of me?

He dreamt that he was still on the aeroplane. He woke up an hour later thirsty, looked up and saw a small arrow painted on the ceiling of the room. What was the arrow for? Out on the balcony, the contrast startled him. Sunset had softened the sky, rimmed the west with pinks and soft orange. The Nile was benign, the sky already revealing a few stars, the air fresher. Birds swooped and zigzagged.

He heard the azan; the first time in his life to hear it outdoors. It was not as spectacular as he had thought it would be, not as sudden. It seemed to blend with the sound of the birds and the changing sky. He started to figure out the direction of Makkah using the setting sun as his guide. Straight east or even a little to the north-east it would be now, not south-east like from Scotland. He located the east and when he went back into the room, understood the purpose of the arrow that was painted on the ceiling. The arrow was to show the hotel guests which way to face Makkah. After he prayed he went downstairs and looked for the swimming pool. He swam in water that was warm and pungent with chlorine. Twilight was swift. In no time the sky turned a dark purple with sharp little stars. It was the first time for him to swim under a night sky.

Her house was larger than he had imagined, shabbier. It was full of people – she had five brothers and sisters, several nephews and nieces, an uncle who resembled an older, smaller version of Bill Cosby and an aunt who was asleep on a string bed in the corner of the room. The television blared. Her mother smiled at him and offered him sweets. Her father talked to him in careful, broken English. Everyone stared at him, curious, pleased. Only the brother looked bored, stretched out on another string bed staring at the ceiling.

So now you've seen my family, she said, naming her sisters, her nieces and nephews. The names swam in his head. He smiled and smiled until he strained the muscles of his face.

Now you've seen where I grew up, she said, as if they had got over a hurdle. He realised for the first time, the things she'd never had; a desk of her own, a room of her own, her own cupboard, her own dressing table, her own mug, her own packet of biscuits. She had always lived as part of a group, part of her family. What was that like? He didn't know. He did not know her well enough. He had yet to see her hair, he had yet to know what she looked like when she cried and what she looked like when she woke up in the morning.

After they had dinner, she said, my uncle knows an English song. She was laughing again, sitting on the arm of the sofa. He wants to sing it for you.

Bill Cosby's look-alike sat up straight in his armchair and sang, *Cricket, lovely cricket at Lords where I saw it. Cricket, lovely cricket at Lords where I saw it.*

Everyone laughed. After singing, the uncle was out of breath.

They went on outings which she organised. They went on a boat trip, a picnic in the forest, they visited the camel market. In each of these outings, they were accompanied by her brother, her sisters, her nephews and nieces, her girlfriends. They were never alone. He remembered Michael in *The Godfather*, climbing the hills of Italy with his fiancé and the unforgettable soundtrack, surrounded by armed guards and her numerous relatives. It was like that but without the guns. And instead of rolling hills, there was flat scrubland, the edges of a desert. He watched her, how she carried a nephew, how she smiled, how she unpeeled a grapefruit and gave him a piece to eat, how she giggled with her girlfriends. He took lots of photographs. She gave him strange fruit to eat. One was called *doum* and it was brown, large as an orange, almost hard as rock, with a woody taste and a straw-like texture. Only the thin outer layer was to be gnawed at and chewed, most of it was the stone. Another fruit was called *gongoleez*, sour, tangy, white chunks, chalky in texture to suck on and throw the black stones away. Tamarind to drink, *kerkadah* to drink, *turmus, kebkebeh, nabaq.* Peanut salad, stuffed aubergines, *moulah, kisra, waikah, mouloukhia.* Dishes he had eaten before in the Nile Café, dishes that were new. She never tired of saying to him, here, taste this, it's nice, try this.

Can't we be alone, just for a bit?

My family are very strict, especially because I'm divorced, they're very strict, she said, but her eyes were smiling.

Try and sort something out.

Next week after the wedding, you'll see me every day and get tired of me.

You know I can't ever get tired of you.

How can I know that?

She could flirt for hours given the chance. Now there was no chance because it was not clear whether her uncle, eyes closed and head nodding forward, was dozing in his armchair or eavesdropping.

Mid-morning in Ghamhouriah Street, after they had bought ebony to take back to his parents, he felt a tug on his shoulder, turned and found his rucksack slashed open, his passport missing. His camera too. He started to shout. Calm down, she said but he could not calm down. It was not only anger – there was plenty of that – but the eruption of latent fears, the slap of a nightmare. Her brother had parked the car in a bit of shade in a side street. They reached it now, her brother tenser than ever, she downcast and he clutching his ravaged rucksack. He kicked the tyre of the car, f– this and f– that. Furious, he was, and out to abuse the place, the time, the crime. The whole street stood still and watched a foreigner go berserk, as if they were watching a scene in an American movie. A car drove past and the driver craned his neck to get a better look, laughed. Please, she said, stop it, you're embarrassing me. He did not hear her. Her voice could not compete with the roar of anger in his ears.

We'll have to go to the British Embassy and get him a new passport, she said to her brother.

No, we'll have to go the police station and report this first. Her brother got in the car, wiped the sweat on his forehead with his sleeves.

Get in the car, she said to him. We'll have to go to the police station and report your stolen passport.

He got in the car, fuming.

The police station was surprisingly pleasant. It was shady, cool. A bungalow and several outbuildings. They were treated well, given cold water, tea. He refused to drink the tea, sat in a sulk. Do you know how much that camera cost, he hissed, and it's not insured?

She shrugged, less shocked by what had happened than he was. Soothed by the drink, she started to tease him. They'll chop off the hand of the thief who stole your camera. Really, they will. Her brother laughed with her.

I really can't see what's so funny.

Can't you take a joke?, she said and there was an edge to her voice. Afterwards they drove in silence to the British Embassy. There, they endured a long queue.

The embassy staff hummed and hawed. They did not like to hear of passports getting stolen. And as one question led to another they were not overjoyed either to hear of people getting married in a few days' time. They interrogated her and her brother, broad, flat questions but still she felt sullied and small.

Coming out of the embassy, she was anything but calm. What did they think, what were they trying to insinuate – that I stole your passport – as if I am desperate to go back there . . . ?

What's that supposed to mean?

It's supposed to mean what it means. You think you're doing me a big favour by marrying me?

No, I don't think that, of course not . . .

They do. They do, the way they were talking. Sneering at me and you didn't even notice!

Okay, okay, calm down.

A small boy touched his arm, begging. Gnarled fist, black skin turned grey from malnutrition, one eye clogged with thick mucous. He flinched at the unpleasant touch, felt guilty, fumbled in his pockets and started to take out a 200-dinar note.

Are you out of your mind, she said, giving him that amount? He'll get mugged for it. She opened her bag and gave the boy instead some coins and an orange.

As she got in the car, she told her brother about the beggar and they both laughed in a mocking way. Laughing at him in Arabic, the height of rudeness.

Perhaps you can contribute to the petrol then, the brother drawled, given you have so much cash to spare. I've burnt a lot of gas chauffeuring you and your fiancé around, you know.

Right, if this is what you want. He yanked out the notes from his wallet and slammed them down near the handbrake.

Thanks, her brother said, but when he picked up the wad of cash, he stared at it like it was not much, like he had expected more.

She sighed and looked out of the window. It was as if the theft had brought out all the badness in them.

He thought of saying, drop me at the hotel. He thought of giving up and leaving for Scotland the next day. That would punish her for laughing at him, that would hurt her. But he did not ask to be dropped off. He did not give up. True, he had no passport and would not be able to travel, but something else made him stay.

They walked into disarray. Her house, almost unrecognisable for the sheer number of people who were distraught, in shock. A woman was pushing the furniture to one side, another dropped a mattress on the floor; everywhere weeping, weeping and a few

137

hoarse voices shouting orders. Her uncle, Bill Cosby, had died, dozing in his armchair.

For a moment, the three of them stood in the middle of the room, frozen in disbelief. The brother started to ask questions in a loud voice.

That's it, she hissed, we'll never have our wedding now, not in the middle of this mourning, never, never. And she burst into tears.

Before he could respond, her brother led him away, saying the house would be for the women now, we have to go outside. Come on.

The garden was hell that time of day, sun scorching the grass, reflecting on the concrete slabs of the garage. How precious shade was in this part of the world, how quickly a quarrel could be pushed aside, how quickly the dead were taken to their graves. Where was he now the uncle who sang *Cricket, lovely cricket?* Somewhere indoors being washed with soap, perfumed and then wrapped in white; that was the end then, without preliminaries. He could faint standing in the sun like this, without a passport, without her, without the reassurance that their wedding would go ahead. It couldn't be true. But it was, and minute after minute passed with him standing in the garden. Where was her brother now, who had previously watched his every move while she had circled him with attention, advice, plans? She was indoors, sucked up in rituals of grief he knew nothing about. Well, he could leave now, slip away unnoticed. He could walk to the main road and hail a taxi – something he had not done before because she and her brother had picked him up and dropped him back at the hotel every single day. Death, the destroyer of pleasures.

The body was being taken away. There it was shrouded in white and the shock of seeing that Bill Cosby face again, asleep, fast asleep. The folds of nostrils and lips, the pleasing contrast of white hair against dark skin. He found himself following her brother into the car, getting into what now had become his seat at the back, two men crammed in next to him, an elderly man sat in front. The short drive to the mosque, rows of men. He had prayed that special prayer for the dead once before in Edinburgh – for a still-born baby. It did not involve any kneeling, was brief, cool. Here it was also raw, the fans whirling down from the ceiling, the smell of sweat and haste.

They drove out of town to the cemetery. He no longer asked himself why he was accompanying them, it seemed the right thing to do. In the car, there was a new ease between them, a kind of bonding because they had prayed together. They began to talk of the funeral announcement that went out on the radio after the news, the obituaries that would be published in the newspaper the next day. He half-listened to the Arabic he could not understand, to the summary in English which one of them would suddenly give, remembering his presence.

Sandy wind blowing, a home that was flat ground, a home that had no walls, no doors. My family's cemetery, her brother said suddenly, addressing him. Once he married her and took her back with him to Edinburgh would he be expected to bring her back here if she, God forbid, died? Why think these miserable thoughts. A hole was eventually made in the ground, you would think they were enjoying the scooping out of dirt, so wholeheartedly were they digging. With the sleeve of his shirt, he wiped the sweat off his brow – he was beginning to act like them – since when did he wipe his face with his shirtsleeves in Edinburgh. He wanted a glass of cold water but they were lowering the uncle in the grave now. They put him in a niche, wedged him in so that when they filled the grave, the soil they poured in did not fall on him.

For the next three days, he sat in the tent that had been set up in the garden for the men. A kind of normality prevailed, people pouring in to pay their condolences, the women going indoors, the men to the tent. A flow of water glasses, coffee, tea, the buzz of flies. Rows of metal chairs became loose circles and knots, as old friends caught up with each other, a laugh here and there could be heard. What's going to happen to your wedding now? he was asked. He shrugged, he did not want to talk about it, was numbed by what had happened, dulled by the separation from her that the mourning customs seemed to impose. In the tent, the men agreed that the deceased had had a good death; no hospital, no pain, no Intensive Care and he was in his eighties, for God's sake, what more do you expect? A strange comfort in that tent. He fell into this new routine. After breakfast in the hotel, he would walk along the Nile, after passing the Presidential Palace, wave down a taxi, go to her house. He never met her and she never phoned him. After spending the day in the tent and having lunch with her brother and his friends, one of them would offer him a lift back to the Hilton.

Late in the evening or the early morning, he would go swimming. Every day he could hold his breath underwater longer. When he went for a walk, he saw army trucks carrying young soldiers in green uniforms. The civil war in the south had gone on for years and wasn't drawing to an end – on the local TV station there were patriotic songs, marches. He had thought, from the books he'd read and the particular British Islam he had been exposed to, that in a Muslim country he would find elegance and reason. Instead he found melancholy, a sensuous place, life stripped to the bare bones.

On the third evening after the funeral, the tent was pulled down; the official mourning period was over.

I want to talk to you, he said to her brother, perhaps we could go for a walk.

They walked in a street calmed by the impending sunset. Only a few cars passed. He said, I can't stay here for long. I have to go back to my work in Scotland.

I'm sorry, the brother said, we could not have your wedding. But you understand . . .

It's going to be difficult for me to come again. I think we should go ahead with our plans . . .

We can't celebrate at a time like this.

It doesn't have to be a big celebration.

You know, she had a big wedding party last time?

No, I didn't know. She didn't tell me.

I blame myself, her brother suddenly blurted out, that son of a dog and what he did to her. I knew, you see, I heard rumours that he was going with that girl but I didn't think much of it, I thought it was just a fling he was having and he'd put his girlfriend away once he got married.

They walked in silence after that, the sound of their footsteps on crumbling asphalt. There was movement and voices in the houses around them, the rustle and barks of stray dogs.

Finally her brother said, I suppose we could have the marriage ceremony at my flat. But just the ceremony, no party . . .

No, no, there's no need for a party . . .

I'll talk to my father and my mother, see if they approve the idea.

Yes, please, and after the ceremony . . . ?

After the ceremony you can take her back with you to your hotel . . .

Right.

Her father has to agree first.

Yes, of course.

He walked lighter now, but there was still another hitch.

You know, her brother said, we lost a lot of money marrying her off to that son of a dog. A lot of money. And now again this time . . . even just for a simple ceremony at my place, I will have to buy drinks, sweets, pay for this and that.

On a street corner, money was exchanged between them. He handed her brother one fifty-dollar bill after the other, not stopping until he sensed a saturation.

Thanks, better not tell her about this, okay? My sister's always been sensitive and she doesn't realise how much things cost.

His hand trembled a little as he put his wallet away. He had previously paid a dowry (a modest one, the amount decided by her) and he had brought the gifts in good faith. Now he felt humiliated, as if had been hoodwinked or as if he had been so insensitive as to under-estimate his share in the costs. Or as if he had paid for her.

On the night before the wedding, he slept lightly, on and off, so the night seemed to him elongated, obtuse. At one time he dreamt of a vivid but unclear sadness and when he woke he wished that his parents were with him, wished that he was not alone, getting married all alone. Where were the stag night, the church wedding, invitation cards, a reception and speeches? His older brother had got married in church wearing the family kilt. It had been a sunny day and his mother had worn a blue hat. He remembered the unexpected sunshine, the photos. He had turned his back on these customs, returned them as if they were borrowed, not his. He had no regrets, but he had passed the stage of rejection now, burnt out the zeal of the new convert, was less proud, more ready to admit to himself what he missed. No, his parents could not have accompanied him. They were not hardy enough to cope with the heat, the mosquitoes, the maimed beggars in the street, all the harshness that even a good hotel could not shield. Leave them be, thank them now humbly in the dark for the generous cheque they had given him.

He dreamt he was being chased by the man who had ripped his rucksack, robbed his passport and camera. He woke up sweaty and thirsty. It was three in the morning – not yet dawn.

He prayed, willing himself to concentrate, to focus on what he was saying, who he was saying it to. In this late hour of the night, before the stir of dawn, all was still even his mind, which usually buzzed with activity, even his feelings, which tumbled young. Just a precious stillness, patience, patience for the door to open, for the contact to be made, for the comforting closeness. He had heard a talk once at the mosque, that there are certain times of the day and the year when Allah answers prayers indiscriminately, fully, immediately – certain times – so, who knows, you might one moment pray and be spot-on, you might ask and straight away be given.

After dawn he slept and felt warm as if he had a fever. But he felt better when he woke late with the phone ringing and her clear voice saying, I'm so excited I'm going to be coming to the Hilton to stay with you. I've never stayed in a Hilton before, I can't wait.

It was a matter of hours now.

Her brother's flat was in a newly built area, a little deserted, out of the way. One of her cousins had picked him up from the hotel and now they both shuffled up the stairs. The staircase was in sand, not yet laid out in tiles or concrete; there was a sharp smell of paint and bareness. The flat itself was neat and simple; a few potted plants, a large photograph of the Ka'ba. The men; her brother, father, various relations and neighbours whom he recognised from the days in the mourning tent, occupied the front room, the one near the door. The women were at the back of the flat. He couldn't see them, couldn't see her.

Shaking hands, the hum of a general conversation in another language. The Imam wore a white jellabiya, a brown cloak, a large turban. He led them for the maghrib prayer and after that the ceremony began. Only it was not much of a ceremony, but a signing of a contract between the groom and the bride's father.

The Imam pushed away the dish of dates that was on the coffee table and started to fill out a form. The date in the western calendar, the date in the Islamic calendar. The amount of dowry (the original figure she had named and not the additional dollars her brother had taken on the street corner). The name of the bride. The name of her father who was representing her. The name of the groom who was representing himself.

But that is not a Muslim name. The Imam put the pen down, sat back in his chair.

Show him your certificate from the mosque in Edinburgh, urged her brother, the one you showed me when you first arrived.

I can't, he said, it was stolen or it fell out when the things in my bag were stolen.

No matter, the brother sighed and turned to speak to the Imam. He's a Muslim for sure. He prayed with us. Didn't you see him praying just now behind you?

Did they tell you I have eyes at the back of my head?

Laughter . . . that didn't last long.

Come on sheikh, one of the guests said, we're all gathered here for this marriage to take place insha' Allah. We've all seen this foreigner praying, not just now but also on the days of the funeral. Let's not start to make problems.

Look, he will recite for you the Fatiha, the brother said, won't you? He put his hand on his shoulder as a way of encouragement.

Come on sheikh, another guest said, these people aren't even celebrating or having a party. They're in difficult circumstances, don't make things more difficult. The bride's brother said he saw an official certificate, that should be enough.

Insha' Allah there won't be any difficulties, someone ventured.

Let him recite, the Imam said, looking away.

He was sweating now. No, not everyone's eyes were on him, some were looking away, hiding their amusement or feeling embarrassed on his behalf. He sat forward, his elbows on his knees.

In the Name of Allah, the Compassionate, the Merciful, her brother whispered helpfully.

In the Name of Allah, the Compassionate, the Merciful, he repeated, his voice hoarse but loud enough. *All praise to Allah, Lord of the*

Worlds and the rest followed, one stammered letter after the other, one hesitant word after the other.

Silence, the scratch of a pen. His hand in her father's hand. The Fatiha again, everyone saying it to themselves, mumbling it fast, raising their palms, Ameen, wiping their faces.

Congratulations, we've given her to you now.

She's all yours now.

When he saw her, when he walked down the corridor to where the women were gathered, when the door opened for him and he saw her, he could only say, oh my God, I can't believe it! It was as if it was her and not her at the same time. Her familiar voice saying his name. Those dark slanting eye smiling at him. But her hair long and falling on her shoulders (she had had it chemically relaxed), make-up that made her glow, a secret glamour. Her dress in soft red, sleeveless, she was not thin . . .

God, I can't believe it! and the few people around them laughed.

A haze in the room, smoke from the incense they were burning, the perfume making him light-headed, tilting his mind, a dreaminess in the material of her dress, how altered she was, how so much more of her there was. He coughed.

Is the incense bothering you?

A blur as someone suggested that the two of them sit out on the balcony. It would be cooler there, just for a while, until they could get a lift to the hotel. He followed her out into a sultry darkness, a privacy granted without doors or curtains, the classical African sky dwarfing the city below.

She did not chat like she usually did. He could not stop staring at her and she became shy, overcome. He wanted to tell her she was beautiful, he wanted to tell her about the ceremony, about the last few days and how he had missed her, but the words, any words, wouldn't come. He was stilled, choked by a kind of brightness.

At last she said, can you see the henna pattern on my palms? It's light enough.

He could trace, in the grey light of the stars, delicate leaves and swirls.

I'll wear gloves, she said, when we go back to Scotland, I'll wear gloves, so as not to shock everyone.

No, you needn't do that, he said, it's lovely.

It was his voice that made her ask. Are you all right, you're not well? She put her hand on his cheek, on his forehead. So that was how soft she was, so that was how she smelt, that was her secret. He said, without thinking, it's been rough for me – these past days – please, feel sorry for me.

I do, she whispered, I do.

Days Rotate

I said, 'Carry me.' He said, 'No.'
  I said, 'Carry me.' He said, 'No.'
So I bit his hand that gripped mine, was leading me. I bit hard
until I cried. His eyes changed from hazel to blue but he didn't let
go. We kept on climbing.

I said, 'Carry me.' He said, 'No.'

I stopped climbing, I stopped moving. Our arms stretched and
the distance lengthened between our eyes. I said, 'This level is fine
for me. I can't go further.'

He said, 'Empty yourself,' and looked away.

I gave up jewelry, a pretty bauble. It smashed on the rocks
below. We kept on climbing.

Cars once drove up this steep mountain path. It is said they
had tyres that gripped the road. Before the Great War there were
lights at night that were neither fire nor the moon. There were
escalators in shopping malls. Astronauts were sent to space. The
earth was a tight, frustrated place. Some died of hunger, some
paid money to lose weight. People were locked up . . . He
remembered the old days, passports and insurance companies,
but I was born in 2115.

He started to sing. I held his voice.

The blows of love play tricks on men
And destroy them stage by stage.
I asked: am I acceptable?
The elders said, Make yourself empty.

We kept on climbing.

Planes once whizzed over this steep mountain path. They sprayed chemicals on the plants. The Great War defeated technology, materialism, the nation state. Now all power was spiritual power, all struggles spiritual struggles. My mother told me about the day in 2114 when the war was won. The babble stopped, no newspapers, radios, TV. In the peace, little voices were heard.

'What is this song?' I asked. He had stopped singing.

'It's from the *diwan* of Sheik Al'Alawi.'

'I'll tell you a riddle,' I said.

'Tell me.'

'Why were Americans good?'

His wide grey eyes, a lilt in his voice, 'I don't know. Why were Americans good?'

'On their money they wrote, "In God we trust".'

He smiled. 'Carry me,' I said. He shook his head. We kept on climbing.

'Tell me about your life before the war,' I said.

'I was covered in a thick rubbery skin, like an elephant's skin. I always wanted more and when I got what I wanted, I quickly became disillusioned with it . . .' His voice made it easier for me to keep on walking.

'Did you own a car?' I wanted details, I was fourteen.

'Yes. A red Porsche.'

'Porsche?'

'A fast car.'

'And what was it like, driving in your fast car?'

'Powerful, fun,' he suddenly stopped walking and I bumped into him, 'But I didn't feel the loneliness because I was coated with that rubber skin.'

I looked up at the sky. Two angels were deep in conversation. Their light made me blink. We kept on climbing.

'How many wives did you have?'

'One. Most men had one wife in the old days.'

'Is she with you now?'

'She died before the war. From cancer.'

'What is cancer?'

'One of the diseases of the past.'

It started to rain. Soft light rain, large flat drops. The rocks began to give thanks, the trees swayed. We slowed down. I stuck my tongue out and tasted rose water. He tipped his head back and tasted aniseed. He took off his turban and let the rain into his hair. His beard became wet. We laughed together.

'Am I your youngest wife?'

'Yes,' his voice as if my question had been irrelevant.

'Why did you not consummate this marriage?'

'You're not ready yet.' He stopped smiling and held my hand again. We climbed. We climbed for miles. The muscles in my legs burned. My eyes were dry from the wind.

I said, 'Carry me,' he said nothing. I said, 'Carry me,' he said nothing. I said, 'I haven't eaten all day, I'm hungry.'

He stopped walking and I saw his eyes change from grey to brown. Heroes of the war were granted the ability to change the colour of their eyes, to cure wounds. He said, 'I'm sorry. I forgot you still needed to eat every day.'

We sat under a tree, in the shadows. He gave me four dates. He took them out of his pocket. I ate three and was too full to eat the fourth. I offered it to him. He shook his head. He only needed to eat every two or three days. It was my youth that made me hungry.

'In the old days it was illegal to marry girls as young as you.' He laughed out loud.

'I don't know what's so funny,' I dug my fingers into the damp soil. I accidentally overturned a snail and apologised. The snail said, 'You didn't break my shell. My shell is pink like your nails.'

The shadow of the tree lengthened over us. When I stood up, my shadow too was equal to my height. The call to prayer came hushed from the snail, muted from the tree, clear and familiar in his voice. Because there was no water to wash, we pressed our palms against the mountain rocks. We rubbed our faces and our arms. He took his *miswak* from his pocket and rubbed his teeth. He said, 'In the old days there were parts of the world where only animals prayed, birds and stones, particles of water and dust. No one could hear them. We were all deaf and busy.' He looked sad when he said that, sadder than I had ever seen him before, his eyes tired, the *miswak* held still in his hand.

I said, 'The old world's passed now. It's over.'

He looked through me and said, 'But days rotate. Days rotate.' I thought of the Freedom Lovers, their slogans and edgy ways.

He put the *miswak* back in his pocket and we began to pray. The ground was cool and wet. Afterwards I wiped mud off his forehead and mine. This made us laugh and we went on climbing.

Steep steps and miles of rough ground. The wind whizzed in my ears. Fatigue. At times my blood burned, at times I was numb, his hand pulling me as if I was walking in my sleep. I said, 'Carry me,' he said, 'No.' I said, 'Carry me,' he said, 'No.'

So I bit his hand, scrunched hair and bone until his eyes turned from brown to blue. He said, 'Empty yourself, you will feel lighter.'

I shouted, 'There is nothing in me anymore.'

'That's not true,' he said. We kept on climbing.

'Carry me.'

'No.'

'Carry me.'

'No.'

'I thought you were my friend!' I pulled my hand away from his and plunged down. I skidded down the slope. It was so easy to go down, to let go, gravity was on my side, helping me. Pebbles rolled along me and I was free. Free of him, free of the struggle of climbing. I laughed out loud and my laugh hit the rock and the trees. A delicious sound: the pleasure of scrunching snails with my feet.

I could go faster now, blind with laughter. Green blur of trees, wind, the spot where we had prayed . . . I slipped and hit my hip against a rock, grazed my face against thistle. So this was how my blood looked, sticky and red. And that buzzing sound . . . I was being cursed by the grass, the thorns, the snails I hadn't killed. They knew my name and complained about me. I looked up and saw two angels move apart, take out pens and start to write. Their light hurt my eyes; I blinked and turned away. But I saw him. I saw him fly. Not like a bird, not like an eagle but as if he had stepped on an invisible escalator. His body still, only the ripple of the wind in his clothes.

'Stand up,' he was now by my side. I thought he was angry but he was out of breath, exerted by the flight, by pressing his will against gravity.

'I can't stand up.'

He knelt next to me, close enough so that I could smell him, watch the colours flicker in his eyes. I had not known that he had reached the level of flight. It was something about him I hadn't known.

'Make me better,' I said. The blood still oozed out from the wound in my knee.

'Cry.'

When I finished crying I stood up and dusted myself.

'Why are we climbing?' he asked, as if I had never ran away, as if I was forgiven.

'I don't know, I don't know. I just want to be with you.'

Then there was so much kindness in his eyes, in the touch of his hand. We started walking.

He sang:

> The blows of love play tricks on men
> And destroy them stage by stage.
> I asked: am I acceptable?
> The elders said, Make yourself empty.
> I know what you mean,
> I replied
> But consider my state
> And show me some compassion,
> Sadness is only the start
> Of the weight I carry.

'Why were there so much troubles in the old world?' I asked.

'People disconnected themselves from Heaven and imagined they could get by.'

'And now?'

'Now the old ways are coming back. There are money lenders charging interest again.'

'I thought these was only market rumours.'

'No, they're true. A loaf of bread only satisfies five people now instead of eight. People are beginning to need more. In some parts of the eastern city, they've taken to locking their homes at night again.'

'My father still keeps an open house.'

'I know.'

'I miss my father,' I said. An ache grew in me for the swing in our courtyard. My sisters and their games. I had twenty brothers and sisters. Some looked like me, some did not look like me at all. My feet dragged on the soil; the memories had made me heavy.

'Now,' he said very gently, 'now, empty yourself.'

I gave up my homeland. It smashed on the rocks below. We kept on climbing.

'A woman once came to my father's house,' I said. 'She knew my name and your name. She knew that we were going to get married. There was something different about this woman. She spoke about power and possession.'

He stopped walking. He turned and I saw green in his eyes and heard the hoofs of horses. He said, 'That woman was one of the Freedom Lovers. They want the world to go back to how it was before. I fought in the Great War so that you can look up at the sky and see angels, so that you can taste roses in the rain and never know famines. We lifted up the grid that separated countries so that people could move about and settle and there would be no border patrols, no immigration laws. But the old ways are creeping back in again. The Freedom Lovers are pushing for another war and I wouldn't put it past them to break the law and use machines.'

'When will that war be?'

'I don't know.'

'In our lifetime?'

He smiled a little, 'I'll teach you how to hold a sword and fight.'

'Who will win us or the Freedom Lovers?'

'Days rotate. Days rotate.'

'What do you mean?'

He paused and I waited. When he spoke he spoke slowly, his eyes dark as purple. 'We were warned from the beginning. We were warned that this mystical life, this contact with Heaven won't last long.'

I wanted him to sing. We kept on climbing.

He said, 'People are needing more sleep now.'

It was true. I now slept five hours each night; last year I only needed four. I said, 'The Freedom Lovers speak about sleep.'

'It's the old ways coming back, tugging like gravity.' His hand did not grip mine as tightly as before.

I sang for him:

> *The blows of love play tricks on men*
> *And destroy them stage by stage.*
> *I asked: am I acceptable?*
> *The elders said, Make yourself empty.*
> *I know what you mean,*
> *I replied*
> *But consider my state*
> *And show me some compassion,*
> *Sadness is only the start*
> *Of the weight I carry.*

He smiled and said that I had a good voice, a clean brain to pick up the words so quickly. He looked at me like that first day in the market. His travelling clothes and the sun on the peppers and aubergines. I knew who he was from his eyes. I went up to him and said, 'I want to offer myself in marriage to you,' and he looked pleased, a little surprised, his eyes moving from hazel to brown like mine. Then I heard his voice for the first time, his accent, 'What is your name?'

We kept on climbing.

I looked up and the sky was purple and faint blue.

We kept on climbing.

I heard a sound, a singing and it was something I had never heard before. It went inside me through my veins. 'What is this? It's so strange.'

'The clouds.'

'Are we nearly there?' The mountain was still solid above us.

He didn't reply. He quickened his step and I was lighter now. He climbed faster and I could keep up. There was no pain. I pushed the ground under my feet. I could see our destination, feel and hear it. Why did I think I could never make it, I could never reach this place? Here was what I had always wanted, every colour and every sound. More beautiful and deep than what I had given up, homeland and jewels. There were tears in his eyes. We had never been so close. I pushed the ground under my feet and it moved. It moved away from me. But that was an illusion, the ground didn't move. We were the ones who were flying.

Radia's Carpet

H e held his father's sword, tried to lift it up but it was still heavy. Too heavy to swing freely or dig in an enemy's chest. He held it with both hands and imagined that the sound of the wind blowing outside the tent was the heave and clash of a battle. A decisive battle like the Battle of Damascus, which clinched the Great War and ended centuries of guns. His father had been martyred in Damascus when Dia' was five years old. Sometimes at night he heard his mother crying, sometimes it was only a dream of the past.

He could hear her now, coming towards the tent. He put the sword away so that she would not say with deliberate encouragement, 'When you're older Dia', you will be able to lift it.' At thirteen he was old enough and they both knew it. Teacher knew it too but he quoted old lines in a comic voice that lifted up Dia's spirits. 'The pen is mightier than the sword,' Teacher would say.

She greeted him when she stepped into the tent, the brown wool of her cape filling the space with warmth. He knew by her voice that something was wrong. 'Radia died,' she said. The sudden sadness made him forget the sword.

'When?'

'During the night, in her sleep.'

He started to cry. The loss of Radia seated on her carpet, flying, the night around her static. He had seen her flying, he had been one of the fortunate ones. Not everyone was so lucky. 'It's because your father is a martyr,' the other children said, the children who had only seen her as an elderly woman, too infirm to do much but sit on her prayer mat. The children believed that Radia could fly, but they had never seen her flying.

'You know what this means, don't you?' His mother took off her cape. She looked younger. Her black hair, wavy like his, was flat over her ears. Her eyes shone with tears or something else.

'What?'

She sighed, 'The carpet.'

'Oh.'

'Radia's carpet?'

'Yes.' He felt uneasy now. His mother intruding too soon, too sudden. He mumbled, 'She's not even buried yet.'

'Teacher put your name forward.' She could not hide it now. The pride in her voice, the hope for her only son.

'Why did he do that?'

'Why did he do that?' His mother mimicked him, came close and kissed him.

'There'll be other competitors,' he said and walked out of the tent.

'Only one,' his mother shouted after him.

Dia' was weeping when he helped the men dig Radia's grave. They dug till the soil was moist and fragrant. Teacher lowered himself into the grave, smoothed with his hand the groove where Radia would lie. He was perspiring and his cloak was streaked with dust and grass. When he finished he wiped his hands on his cloak and held up his arms as if he wanted Dia' to jump into them. Gently and slowly, the men gave him Radia, swathed in white cloth, light and he laid her down. He paused a little, then climbed out of the grave and the men started to scoop the soil back to fill the grave, their spades scratching and ringing in the silence. Before they finished Teacher said, 'Look!'

Dia' stopped crying. He looked and saw flowers start to grow around Radia, pink, white and orange flowers so that in a few seconds she was lying in a garden, not in a grave.

'I found out who the other competitor is,' his mother said when he came back home.

'Who?'

'Taghreed.'

'Oh.'

'Oh,' his mother mimicked him.

'Maybe Radia's carpet should go to a girl. It would be fair – from one woman to another.'

His mother stuck out her chin in disapproval. 'It's for the king to decide.'

Dia' started to walk out again. He wanted the sky. His mother's voice followed him, 'And she put her own name forward, Taghreed did. A tough girl . . .'

He lay flat on the grass and stared up at the sky. 'Take me, take me,' he whispered and the clouds laughed back, teasing him.

Taghreed. Yes, he knew her well from school. She could not sit still. She worked, she cleaned, she spoke out, she could not be still. He had always felt uneasy in her presence, her sharp eyes, her quickness. But she had said to him once, 'You are mild and this is a worthy quality.' She had looked at him strangely then as if she liked him and he had escaped from her intensity, stumbling from the schoolroom to the sky outside.

So he and Taghreed were to stand before the king and compete for Radia's flying carpet. Why were he and Taghreed eligible? Because they had seen Radia fly – they were the only children who had seen Radia fly. And how had that happened? Taghreed had had the audacity to walk up to Radia one day and demand to see her in flight. And Dia'? His father had been martyred in Damascus and this was why, everyone agreed, Radia had revealed herself to him – in honour of his father.

In the days before the audience with the king, his mother cooked Dia' his favourite food. He ate and dreaded her coming disappointment. The more she sparkled with hope, the more his heart sank. He had said to her a number of times, 'A woman's carpet should be passed on to a woman,' gently preparing her for his defeat. But she had repeatedly brushed off his words. 'It's for the king to decide.' She looked very beautiful and confident these days, unsuited to the bareness of the tent. They could not afford a house of bricks, or even a mud house like the one Taghreed lived in.

It had always been Dia's wish that his mother would remarry and he would then have a stepfather, a brick house. He specifically wished that she would marry Teacher. That would strengthen the bond between them; they would become more than pupil and teacher. But Teacher already had four wives, all in the best of health. Dia' had prayed for the death of one of them to make room for his mother. Not any one of them but the third wife. She was lean and agile, with boyish eyebrows and lips that rarely spoke or smiled. She possessed neither the beauty of the first wife, nor the motherliness of the second nor the fun-loving nature of the fourth. Dia' had seen her compete in the Women's Archery Championship and win. Her skill had filled him with envy, the kind of envy that brought tears and bile and hatred of himself. A poisonous arrow would kill her, he had fantasised in class one day and this deep dark wish for someone's death had taken shape, the shape of a bat-like creature which flew around the class, stinking the air and making the girls (all except Taghreed) shriek. Teacher killed it with his dagger, pinned it yelping to the blackboard. Its blood dripped through a drawing of the position of the closer stars. It was Taghreed who washed the blackboard afterwards, while Dia' and Teacher went outside to bury the dead, heavy beast in the sunlit schoolyard. It relieved Dia' to put it under the ground. And Teacher did not demand to know the truth. Instead he talked to Dia' about his name: Dia' meaning glow. Teacher talked as if they were not in any hurry to go back into the class. He talked about radiance, about luminosity, the rays of the sun, the light of dying stars and how there were many, many many darknesses and only one Light. For a whole hour Teacher talked and Dia' absorbed. It turned out to be one of the happiest hours of Dia's life, the badness buried like a turd and Teacher's voice telling him about light.

'Eat, eat,' his mother kept saying on the day before the audience with the king. She herself could eat nothing. She was too excited.

He was full of her food when he stood before the king. The king had fought in Damascus and now his eyes, when he studied Dia' and Taghreed, deepened from blue to purple to black. If Dia's father had survived the war he too would have been a hero like the king, granted the ability to change the colour of his eyes.

The court was as spacious as the sea, as powerful and now serene. The king's beard was like Teacher's but his voice was more beautiful, his accent more refined. He said, 'There are seven flying carpets in the world. They remain with their owners till death, then they are passed on. It is understandable that your village wants to continue to possess the blessing of the carpet. But if both of you fail today, I will have no choice but to give the children of another village the chance to compete for this carpet. Now reflect before you speak.'

He began the questions. Thousands heard the questions, Dia's replies, Taghreed's replies, there was no privacy that day. The first questions were easy. Why was the Great War fought? What did it

161

bring an end to? Material power. What took its place? Spiritual power. How tall were the people of the past? What is the distance between Uranus and Montar? This Taghreed knew and Dia' didn't. How long did the father of humanity live? Dia' said, one thousand years. But Taghreed knew the correct answer, nine hundred and sixty years.

When Dia' looked at Taghreed he saw that she looked scrubbed, alert, on her guard. The king's eyes changed colour but remained sad. I am sorry, Dia' wanted to say to him, I am sorry my father was martyred and you were not, I am sorry. But the questions rolled from the king one after the other like waves, his eyes lightening from purple to azure.

'What is your ego?'

Dia answered, 'My ego is as big as the moon and just as familiar.'

Taghreed said, 'My ego is a statue, its curves moulded by my own hand.'

'What does the best teacher teach?'

'Reign in your ego, ride it, don't let it ride you.'

'Reign in your ego, ride it, don't let it ride you.'

'How should the pupil reply?'

'I do my best. Work very hard.'

'I love you, Teacher.'

'Tell me something wrong you have done; none of us is blameless.'

She said, 'I was so angry once I couldn't see. I picked up a kitchen knife and dug it in a tree. When the tree winced from pain, I cried over it in regret. The background of sin is blindness that is red and hot.'

'I stole a bottle of bubbles,' Dia' said. 'At first my conscience pricked me then I let the feeling of guilt subside. The background of sin is a blur and smoke.'

'What does the devil say?'
Taghreed answered, 'He says, "I am worthy of respect".'
Dia' answered, 'He says, "Eat from both the allowed and the forbidden. They are the same." '

'Why do you deserve Radia's carpet?' the king finally asked.
'I am a woman like Radia. I want to fly.'
'It will make my mother happy. She is lonely and poor.'

When the decision was announced, Dia' felt Taghreed wince and wrap her strength around her to smooth over the disappointment. But the pain was in her eyes for all to see, a broken look that did not suit her. She had wanted the carpet too much. Too much to be in awe of it. And the king only handed out power to those who didn't want it.

'Will you still like me?' Dia' asked her in a whisper, his tongue loose and reckless from victory.

She did not reply.

He did not have time to question her uncharacteristic silence because his mother pounced on him and hugged him and wept and then threw herself at the king's feet, hugging his calves and madly kissing his shoes. This outburst restored Taghreed and Dia' to their normal selves. Taghreed firmly led his distraught mother away and Dia' plunged back into silence and scorn for himself.

Their homecoming was triumphant but raw from parting with the king. His mother must clutch the precious carpet, show it to everyone, laugh with the sheer delight of being for once envied rather than pitied. Teacher exaggerated by slaughtering a camel and feeding hundreds and boasting of his pupil. Even his third wife sang a song about a new dress. The excitement lasted well into the night until exhaustion took over and everyone slept. Everyone except Dia'. The carpet was blue and smooth under his feet. When he knelt down, he breathed in a musk that made him dizzy. It took him by surprise how pliant the carpet was, how ready to give up itself to him; an intimacy that made him smile.

Acknowledgements

Some of the stories in this collection have appeared elsewhere:

'Coloured Lights' in *Chapman* and was broadcast on BBC Radio 3.

'Souvenirs', *New Scottish Writing 1997* (Flamingo, 1997).

'Visitors' was broadcast on BBC Radio 4 and the BBC World Service.

'Tuesday Lunch,' *Special Reserve*, ed. Yvonne Spence (Scottish Cultural Press, 1996).

'The Museum', *Ahead of its Time*, ed. Duncan McLean (Jonathan Cape, 1997) and reprinted in *Opening Spaces*, ed. Yvonne Vera (Heinemann, 1999).

'Majed', *New Writing Scotland 17*, eds Moira Burgess and Donny O'Rourke (ASLS, 1999) and reprinted in *Wasafiri*.

'Something Old, Something New' *Scottish Girl About Town*, Pocket Books 2003.

'Baby Love' *Wasafri*', issue 42, 2004.

By the same author

THE TRANSLATOR

'She covered her hair with Italian silk, her arms with tropical colours. She wanted to look as elegant as Benazir Bhutto, as mesmerising as the Afghan princess she had once seen on TV wearing hijab, *the daughter of an exiled leader of the* mujahideen'

Sammar is a young Sudanese widow working as an Arabic translator in a British university. Following the sudden death of her husband, and estranged from her young son, she drifts – grieving, isolated and exiled from the warmth and colours of her home.

Slowly life returns when she finds herself falling in love with Rae, a Scottish academic. Twice divorced and a self-proclaimed cynic, to Sammar he seems to come from another world. Separated by culture and faith, but drawn to each other, this is a story about love, both human and divine.

'A pattern was set . . . every arrival to Africa was similarly accompanied by loss or pain, a blow to his pride. Baggage disappearing, nights spent in quarantine, stolen travellers' cheques. As if from him the continent demanded a forfeit, a repayment of debts from the ghosts of the past.'

ISBN 1 904598 54 4   £8.99